SHATTERED VOWS

SUSAN K. DRONEY

This is a work of fiction. Names, characters, places, and incidents are products of the author's imagination or are used fictitiously and are not to be construed as real. Any resemblance to actual events, locations, organizations, or persons, living or dead, is entirely coincidental.

World Castle Publishing, LLC
Pensacola, Florida
Copyright © Susan K. Droney 2019
Paperback ISBN: 9781951642006
eBook ISBN: 9781951642013
First Edition World Castle Publishing, LLC, November 18, 2019
http://www.worldcastlepublishing.com

Licensing Notes
Cover: Karen Fuller
Editor: Maxine Bringenberg

CHAPTER ONE

Farrel locked the bathroom door and then quickly turned on the fan and the cold-water tap. She watched the basin fill and turned off the tap, dipped a washcloth into the cold water, and then pressed the cloth against her right eye, wincing with pain as she held it there for a few minutes. Farrel willed her mind to go blank — anything to erase the scene that had transpired less than five minutes ago. She didn't dare raise her eyes to the mirror above the sink — not yet. She needed time to think up an excuse for her latest *accident*.

Farrel slumped, defeated, to the floor, giving in to her emotions. She winced again when a salty tear slid down her raw cheek. What was she going to do? Where could she go? Was it really her fault? Robert always warned her not to make him angry. He constantly reminded her that he was the head of the household and, as his wife, she was to submit to him without question. There was no middle ground. She had no idea what had prompted his outburst this time. When he came home from work, she'd had his favorite meal on the table, the apartment was spotless, and their three teenagers were on their best behavior.

Deep down, Farrel knew Robert really didn't need a reason to abuse her. If he had a bad day at work, she was his punching bag. He relieved his frustrations by taking them out on her. Sometimes he only verbally abused her, and then he would question why she had no self-esteem and lovingly tell her she was a wonderful wife and mother. From abuse to compliments she'd gotten caught up in the middle, and lately had begun to question her own sanity. Perhaps she really was a terrible human being. Maybe deep down Robert was right. Had she deserved the abuse? Farrel felt like a failure in everything she did. No wonder her family and friends had deserted her. Robert was her only friend. She had Robert and the kids. That was all. Her life was a mess, and all she had to show for thirty-five years of life was a long list of failures.

Farrel pulled herself to her feet and forced herself to look at her reflection in the mirror. A stranger stared back at her. *That can't be me*, she thought. Her eye was puffy and turning a horrible shade of purple. Robert's ring had left a gash in her right cheek. She sighed as she performed her usual ritual of applying makeup to cover her injuries, then ran a brush through her long blonde hair.

A faint tapping sounded on the door. She set the brush down, hoping it wasn't Robert.

"Mom, it's me," a shaky voice called from the other side of the door. "Are you okay?"

Farrel quickly unlocked the door to face her first-born. Frankie stared in horror as sobs shook her thin body. "Mom," she whimpered. "How can you put up with this?"

Farrel put her arms around her daughter and held her close for a few seconds, at the same time hating herself for letting her daughters be witnesses to Robert's violence. She released Frankie and held her at arm's length. Frankie was a beauty at the tender age of sixteen. Silky blonde hair framed her delicate face. Farrel was looking at a carbon copy of herself at that age. The only difference was that her child lacked the carefree whimsy most girls her age should feel. The same carefree teenager that Farrel herself had once been, but had allowed to be denied to her daughter. She could never forgive herself for what she'd allowed her daughters to endure.

Frankie reluctantly went out with her friends to do the things most teenagers did only because Farrel insisted. But Farrel knew her daughter couldn't truly enjoy herself, because Frankie had confided in her several times that she worried about her mother when she was away from her. Frankie was frightened because she never knew what she would find when she returned home. It wasn't normal. Farrel knew that, and it added to her own insecurities about the kind of mother she was by subjecting her daughters to this life. She wanted Frankie to enjoy her teenage years with all the hopes and dreams of a wonderful future to look forward to.

Farrel swallowed the lump in her throat as she looked into Frankie's eyes. She couldn't bear the pain in the eyes staring back at her. A good mother would never let her children be witness to Robert's viciousness. A good mother would have left him and provided her children with a safe and happy environment. Did her children understand why she couldn't leave? Did she even understand?

Gary Blackmon, the most popular boy in school, had recently asked Frankie to a high school dance. For weeks Frankie had talked about nothing but Gary; how kind he was, how handsome he was with his wavy black hair and coal-black eyes. For the first time in a long time, Farrel had felt relief that maybe her daughters would be okay. Maybe they could enjoy a normal future after all, and be unscathed by what they had been put through. She'd been thrilled when Frankie had shared her good news with her, but she'd been dismayed when she saw the familiar doubt in Frankie's eyes.

Why would the most popular boy in school, who could have his pick of any girl, ask *her* out? Robert had been successful at chipping away at Frankie's self-esteem, too.

Farrel had listened patiently as Frankie tried to convince herself that maybe Gary only asked her out because he felt sorry for her. When Farrel tried to impress upon her daughter how beautiful she was and the many fine attributes she possessed, Frankie would not be swayed and accused Farrel of telling her those things out of a sense of obligation as her mother. After all, Frankie reasoned, no mother would tell her daughter she was ugly even if that was the case.

Farrel knew that Frankie's self-esteem was at a lower ebb than she'd realized. Her daughter's lack of self-worth was Ferrel's fault. Robert's abuse had affected all of them and would continue to do so unless she changed things. Farrel was the only one who could change the paths of their lives. She also worried that her daughters would either become involved with abusive men or be afraid to make a normal commitment to any man. She felt the weight of the world on her shoulders.

"Mom, can't you just leave Robert? You, Charly, and I were happy before. We can't stand Robert," she said through gritted teeth. "This is the 1990s, not the 1950s when men never got in trouble for beating their wives. We need to leave," Frankie insisted in a quivering voice. "Or have him arrested. Do something, Mom. Please?"

"I'll think of something, honey. I promise." She didn't know what to do, but something had to change, and she was the only one who could do it. She smiled weakly. "Where's Charly?"

"Robert made her go to her room. He said he was sick of her backtalk." Frankie's eyes filled with tears as she put a delicate hand to her mother's cheek.

"Where's Bobby?" Farrel asked.

She shrugged her shoulders. "I don't know. Robert said he was going to take him somewhere." Her lips tightened. "I wonder what he'll come back with this time. It's not fair, Mom!"

"No, it's not, Frankie," she answered softly as she again wondered what she could do. "I've got an idea," she said, trying to lighten the mood. "Let's get Charly and watch an old movie. Just the three of us, like old times. I'll even make some popcorn." She smiled.

Hours later, Farrel lay in the king-sized bed she shared with her husband. She desperately wanted to fall into a deep sleep and be swept away to that place where she was protected and loved. Only her dreams provided her with the life she yearned for — the safe place in her subconscious where her husband adored her and her children. But sleep didn't come, and she was faced with the cold, harsh truth of what her life really was. This was her reality.

She lay in bed, trying to focus on the positives of her life. There had to be some. No, the only bright spot was her daughters. They were all she lived for. They deserved so much more out of life. She'd long ago given up on finding any happiness for herself but wanted her daughters to have everything that had been denied her. Her girls needed her to be strong. They needed her to set the example they would follow. She couldn't let them down.

The hell she was living was worse than death. Slowly, over the years, parts of herself had passed away, victim of a long and painful death. Farrel had been unaware of it until one day she didn't know herself anymore. The smile and forced happiness she showed to the world was just a mask covering the person she'd become. All that was left was a hollow shell.

Farrel could never bring back the happy, fun-loving person she had once been. The past four years had murdered that person, and she could not raise herself from the dead. It was her fault for the mistakes she'd made. No one had forced her to marry Robert. She'd put her daughters and herself into this situation. If only she could turn back time. Farrel wondered what kind of life she would be living. She envisioned it would be in a happy marriage where her children were loved and felt safe and protected. Fantasizing didn't change her current situation. She sighed. She was mentally defeated.

An hour earlier, she'd heard Robert's key in the lock, and listened as he shuffled down the hall to Bobby's room. Bobby talked animatedly about some extravagant purchase his father had gotten him. Farrel sighed. It would mean juggling the monthly budget again.

She felt sick to her stomach. After one of her husband's outbursts, he always took Bobby out for a trip to the mall. He never asked her children to come along. His excuse was always the same: *My boy comes first with me. I'm not the girls' real father.* Tears stung her eyes. She loved her daughters with all of her heart and soul, and she tried to love Bobby, but as time wore on, he was turning into a duplicate of his father. He could be so sweet and loving when he was alone with her but turned into an obnoxious beast when his father was around. Bobby knew how to pull his father's strings and enjoyed playing him against her. He was going to grow up to repeat his father's actions in his own relationships. That fact broke her heart. It was a vicious cycle, and she was caught up in the middle of it, but with no power to end it.

To bring Bobby's behavior to his father's attention would

only incite another outburst from Robert against her and her daughters. Farrel remembered Robert saying over and over that he and his son had no faults, but always had to deal with everyone else's. It was a hopeless situation.

She heard the bedroom door quietly open. She took a deep breath as she heard Robert remove his clothes and slip into bed beside her.

"Hi, sweetheart," he said as he nuzzled her shoulder with his chin. He planted tender kisses on her neck.

Farrel struggled to hold back her tears. Why couldn't her husband be this gentle all of the time? This same scene played out over and over after his abuse. She had it memorized. Robert would act as though nothing had happened, and even express surprise at her bruises and deny responsibility for her injuries. His excuse would be that she happened to be in his way and stumbled, or that she was imagining the abuse and then feign shock that she could ever think he would hurt her. Robert even offered to help her find a counselor for the mental and emotional problems he insisted she had. Sometimes she wondered if she was losing her mind. Her daughters witnessed many of his attacks, but his answer was always the same. They were lying about him because they hated him and wanted to make him look like a monster to the world. Farrel knew that somewhere within himself, he knew his guilt. He had to.

Robert brushed her hair from her brow. The moonlight cast just enough light over the bed to illuminate them. "You are so beautiful," he whispered as he caressed her neck and then slowly and masterfully slid his hands down to her breasts.

Farrel wanted to squelch the fire beginning inside of her as he skillfully manipulated her body into raw sexual passion. She pleaded with herself to remember what he had done to her only hours earlier. Her heartbeat quickened as her uncontrollable passion melted into the depths of his body. He continued to sexually tease her until he could no longer contain his own desire.

<<<>>>

Later Farrel listened to Robert's steady rhythmic breathing and knew that he was sound asleep. She gently touched his cheek and stared down at him. He looked so peaceful and innocent, almost boyish, lying with one leg kicked out from under the blanket. A strand of jet-black hair fell loosely over his brow.

Farrel ached to get inside his mind to learn where his violence came from. How could he love her so passionately one minute, then physically and verbally abuse her the next? Every time she convinced herself that she should leave him, it seemed as though he could read her mind, and he would suddenly do an about-face and act sweet and attentive, convincing her that she should give him one more chance. Deep down, she knew that her fear of leaving him really stemmed from the fact that she had nowhere to go and no one to help her. But at the same time, she wondered how many more chances she could give him before he completely destroyed her.

Farrel got out of bed, walked over to the window seat, and sat down, drawing her slender legs to her chin. She stared out into the silent darkness. She longed to be a child again when she'd felt safe and protected against all the harsh cruelties of the world. That was so long ago before her life had become so complicated. Farrel gazed at a bright star and thought of how many times she had wished upon a star as a child, and with a child's innocence, had believed that her wish would be granted.

She still felt the touch of Robert's masculine hands. Farrel breathed deeply, wishing for some normalcy to her life. She craved to be loved and cherished. Robert satisfied her sexually but left her feeling cold and empty inside. "Please, God," she prayed, "let my husband see what he is doing, and help him to change." Farrel hugged her knees as her body trembled and silent tears began to fall.

<<<>>>

Farrel was standing at the stove, fixing Robert's breakfast when he entered the small kitchen. He walked over to the table and set his briefcase down with a loud thud next to his chair, then firmly planted his hands on the back of the chair.

The girls had been chatting as they ate, but now abruptly fell silent. Farrel noticed the chilly silence and slightly turned her head and stole a glance at her husband. Robert was impeccably dressed in black slacks and a gray jacket. His jaw was firmly set, and his facial expression caused an icy coldness to creep up her spine. Her hand trembled slightly as she turned back to the stove and flipped the pancakes. She drew a deep breath and slowly turned to face him. "Good morning, honey," she said, trying to keep her voice bright. "Are you going to be late tonight?"

"I don't know," he said as his eyes swept over her face.

Farrel saw the disgust in his eyes. This morning she'd tried to mask her bruises, but the ugly purple welt on her cheek showed through, and her eye was a sickening shade of black and blue.

"What did you run into this time?" he asked sharply, rolling his eyes.

She fought the urge to retort, "Your fist," but instead said, "I don't know. Maybe the cupboard." Farrel looked at her daughters. She could read no emotion on their faces. They knew it was useless to contradict anything Robert said. He was the ultimate authority.

"You sure are clumsy, Farrel," Bobby laughed.

Bobby knew the truth. He had seen what his father had done to her last night. Her jaw tightened, but she kept her silence. Bobby was a husky boy for his fifteen years, and tall. Most people took him to be at least a couple of years older. His hair color was the same as his father's, and he had those same penetrating dark eyes, eyes that she knew hid so much of the truth behind them. She turned back to the stove, fighting to keep her composure.

Robert walked over to her and roughly clamped his hands on her shoulders, causing her to wince in pain. "Don't you ever look at my son like that again!" he thundered.

"I...I didn't," she said lamely, then added, "But I wish you would have him show some respect for me."

He laughed loudly. "Respect!" He turned to his son. "Son, she wants your respect!"

Bobby smirked as he finished his bowl of cereal. "You sure know how to pick 'em, Dad."

Robert turned her around. "How can you have the nerve to ask anyone to respect you? Look at yourself. You can't do anything right. It's a wonder you can even dress yourself in the morning!"

Tears stung her eyes as she stole a glance at Frankie and Charly. Farrel saw the pain in their eyes, and it shattered her heart. She had to do something, but she didn't know what. Her head throbbed. Farrel looked into her husband's cold, black eyes. "Honey, let me turn off the stove." She kept her voice light, masking her inner turmoil.

He released his grip on her. "Get my breakfast!"

She heaped pancakes on a plate and handed them to him. "I made them just the way you like them." She smiled faintly.

Robert looked at the pancakes and slammed the plate on the counter. "You don't know how to do anything just the way I like it." He walked over to the table, picked up his briefcase, and left the room without another word.

Minutes later, Farrel heard the front door slam. Trying to make sense out of Robert's moods frustrated her. She never knew what would set him off, but it seemed that it had everything to do with her. She'd never please him no matter what she did for him. Nothing ever changed. She had to face the truth…it never would.

After the children left for school, Farrel occupied herself for the remainder of the morning with doing her daily household chores. She walked from room to room of the cramped apartment as though in a daze, wondering why her life had turned out completely opposite of what she had planned. Farrel sat on the edge of her bed, put her head in her hands, and closed her eyes. She tried to pray but found no peace. She felt like God had deserted her, too, and doubted she would ever feel peace again.

At noon Farrel went outside to weed the small garden she had planted a couple of weeks earlier. Each tenant in the apartment complex was allotted a small plot of land each spring for flowers or vegetables. She pulled the weeds, enjoying the mid-May sunshine splashing down on her back. She was aware of the chatter between her neighbors as they brought out lawn chairs for their daily visits while basking in the warmth of the beautiful day. Farrel caught bits and pieces of their conversations and longed to be included in their circle of friendship, but knew it could never happen. When she and Robert had moved in two years earlier, he had forbidden her from getting chummy with their new neighbors. Farrel didn't blame her neighbors for ignoring her because she'd shrugged off all attempts at friendship, so they'd left her alone, assuming that was what she wanted. She wondered what the neighbors really thought about her. She must seem odd to them, staying so withdrawn in her own little world with just Robert and the kids. Farrel was certain they heard plenty coming from the apartment because of the paper-thin walls. Whenever she passed one of the women in the hallway, she noticed a curious, wondering look, but no one ever tried to initiate anything beyond a greeting since Farrel had rebuked their neighborly gestures so many times before. How she wished someone would see the loneliness welled up inside her. Couldn't someone see how desperately she needed a friend?

Farrel kept her head low, perspiration beading up on her forehead. Sweat trickled down her back, but she continued working, immersed in her private thoughts, and didn't hear approaching footsteps.

"Good afternoon, Mrs. Drake. It's a beautiful day, isn't it?" a pleasant voice asked.

Farrel jumped, startled, and then quickly regained her composure. "Yes, it is," she answered shyly, still keeping her head bent low.

"I didn't mean to frighten you. I was just admiring your garden. You seem to know an awful lot about vegetable plants. I was wondering if you could give me a few hints." The woman laughed as she continued, "My garden looks sick compared to yours. Bill, my husband, said I should talk to you."

Farrel slowly raised her head and looked into the older woman's friendly face. Her eyes met the woman's, and she saw the shock in them as they swiftly looked over Farrel's bruises. She pulled herself to her feet. "I'd be happy to help." Farrel wiped her hands on the back of her jeans.

She followed the woman to a plot a few feet away and almost laughed out loud when she saw the tangled mass of weeds and plants. She dug into the moist soil and yanked at the weeds.

"By the way, my name is Betty Levitt. I've lived here for over twenty years," the woman said in a cheery tone of voice.

"It's nice to meet you. I'm Farrel Drake," Farrel timidly replied.

"I know," the woman said with a smile. "Your husband's name is Robert, and he's a sales representative for Automon Plastics. You have three children...two girls and a boy."

Farrel became uncomfortable as she wondered how much more the woman knew about her. Betty Levitt didn't dig for information, but still, Farrel felt the need to make up an excuse for her bruises. "I must be the clumsiest person alive," she finally said. "Last night, I ran right into a cupboard door. I guess one of the kids forgot to close it." She frowned.

"It happens to the best of us. How about coming up to my apartment for a cup of coffee?" Betty offered.

"I wish I could, but I have a lot to do this afternoon," Farrel lied. She fought back the urge to accept the invitation because she so desperately longed for a friend, someone to share her deepest thoughts with. But she knew what would happen if she disobeyed Robert and he was to find out. He warned her repeatedly that people would interfere in their lives if she involved herself in any womanly friendships — or *cat sessions*, as he referred to them. Of course, it didn't matter that he had several family members and co-workers in whom he confided, but, as he pointed out, he was a man, and that was the difference.

"How about tomorrow morning then? After your husband and kids get off to work and school? A few of us women get together to swap recipes and just have some plain old-fashioned girl talk. It's about time that we got to know you," Betty said.

Farrel hesitated. "I don't know, Mrs. Levitt."

"Betty."

"Okay, Betty. I'll get back to you later." She offered a weak smile.

"Good enough."

Farrel wondered how she could keep Betty Levitt at a distance. If the woman sensed Farrel was evading her, she didn't let on. She wanted more than anything to be included in Betty's friendly circle, but even more than that, she feared Robert's retribution if she opposed his authority.

CHAPTER TWO

Farrel sat at the kitchen table, intently writing in a notebook. The table was strewn with scraps of paper, pens, and envelopes.

"The famous author is at it again," Robert mocked as he leaned against the refrigerator watching her.

She smiled. "It's in my blood, honey. I can't help it... it's what I've always wanted to do. Maybe someday I'll be published." She shrugged. "If not, I'll still continue writing."

"All I can see is a waste of my hard-earned money, Farrel."

His words stung, but she ignored his comment.

Robert walked to the table, pulled out a chair, and sat down across from her. "So, what do you write about, anyway?"

Farrel set her pen down. "You've never seemed interested before," she said, surprised.

"I didn't say I was interested. Just curious."

She sighed. Why did he have to try to ruin everything that meant something to her? She wanted so much to be able to have the kind of normal relationship where they could share their individual passions with one another. She looked at him. He was dressed in an old paint stained shirt and faded jeans. His feet were bare. His attire was unusual, but she didn't dare question it. "Mostly, I write about my feelings. Sometimes what I'm feeling pours out on paper and releases all of my frustrations. The difference is that I can control my characters so they can have the most wonderful lives with all of their dreams fulfilled."

Robert's eyes narrowed. "Are you saying that your life isn't satisfying to you?"

Farrel noticed the disapproval in his eyes as he swept over her makeup-less face and uncombed hair. Self-consciously she swept a strand of hair from her brow as she pondered his question. "No, I don't mean to imply that. It's just that everyone always wishes certain aspects of their lives were different. In my writing, I can fulfill all of my dreams through my characters' actions and emotions."

Robert stared at her and sniffed. "It doesn't make any sense to me—just a waste of my money and your time, which you could be spending fixing up this dump!"

Farrel glanced around the room. "The house is clean, Robert. I can't help it that this apartment is too small for five people. It's cluttered, but not dirty." Her eyes grew bright. "If I could just get one book into the right hands, I could be on my way. I could help to support us. With your income, the child support for the girls, and money from the book, we could buy a house and be able to afford a few luxuries."

He laughed. "You live in a dream world."

"No, you don't understand, honey. I know I can write. I just wish I could explain it to you. It's not a waste of time or money. Most writers have been rejected numerous times, but they never gave up their dream. I need you to support me in this. I know that someday it's going to happen for me. I can feel it, Robert. I have the ability to create any situation I want," she said enthusiastically.

He smirked. "You're right about one thing. You do have the ability to create situations. Maybe if you spent more time thinking about your family's needs and less time on some stupid dream of becoming a writer, which I personally believe will never happen, things would be better between us," he said sarcastically as he glared at her. "Why don't you put something decent on instead of running around like a slob?" He stood up. "One more thing...when you show me some money, maybe I'll take this foolishness seriously."

Tears stung her eyes. "Everyone has to have a dream. If we didn't have our dreams, life would be pretty dull." She chewed her bottom lip. "There would be nothing to look forward to."

"Reality, Farrel. You have to face reality. You will *never* be a famous author. And if you believe in the Lord, as you claim, you should not be seeking after worldly pleasures."

Her face flushed. "That's what you don't understand. The Lord gave me this ability, Robert. We should use our talents to the best of our ability. I have this passion to write, and it came from the Lord," she explained. "And I never said anything about being famous. I don't seek fame. I'd only like to be able to earn enough to give us what we can't afford."

"The Lord also commands that I am the head of the household, and you are to be in complete submission to me," he stated firmly.

Anger rose rapidly to the surface, and Farrel drew a deep breath and held it at bay. "Sometimes you twist things, Robert. The Lord gave me my own mind. I don't see what harm my writing is doing. Writing is something of my own, and there is nothing wrong with me wanting to be a writer."

Robert laughed as he shook his head. "You are such a fool. You're doing a terrible injustice to the Lord with your crazy dream."

"No, I'm not! I don't see where you're so perfect, Robert!"

She knew she should have kept her mouth shut, but like a mother protecting her young, she was defending the only part of herself she had left. "What do you think you're showing the Lord?" she shouted, immediately sorry for her last remark as she awaited his reaction.

He rubbed his chin and then slowly picked up a handful of her papers and shuffled through them. He selected a page and began to read to himself for a few minutes. Farrel sat quietly, watching him, but couldn't tell what he was thinking. His face showed no emotion one way or the other.

Suddenly, he raised his eyes and stared contemptuously at her. He grabbed a pile of loose sheets, tore them in half, and then tore them again before depositing them in the wastepaper basket. "Unbelievable!"

She watched in horror. "What are you doing?" she cried. "Robert, please...no!"

"I'm putting this garbage where it belongs," he hissed as he reached for another stack of papers.

Her heart thudded as she grabbed his wrist. "Don't!" she screamed. "You have no right. That's my personal property!"

His hand froze in mid-air, and his head snapped around. "Don't you *ever* grab my wrist or question my authority again!"

Farrel released him. She knew what was coming. Her insides began to quiver as she waited for her punishment.

Robert slowly stood up and walked around the table. He stopped abruptly behind her chair and stood quietly for a few seconds.

Farrel's heart banged against her chest. She was terrified to turn around. The seconds ticked by. *What is he thinking? What is he going to do?* She sat without moving a muscle, as though she were glued to the chair.

Robert gruffly grabbed a fistful of her hair and pulled on it, bringing her to her feet. He spun her around until she was facing him. "Do you want to be treated like a whore?" he demanded. "Like the women you write about?"

He held her so close that she could feel his warm breath on her face. "I don't write about women like that," she answered in a small voice.

"Why do you write such trash?"

"It's not trash. If you read the whole thing, you would see that it is nothing more than a love story."

"Sure," he sneered. "Where are the kids?"

"They should be home pretty soon. You know how teenagers are." She looked at him, wondering what to expect.

"You baby the girls too much, Farrel, and I'm sick and tired of it."

Farrel wondered where his emotions would take him next. It was difficult to gauge his outbursts. Sometimes he went from one subject to another without warning. She'd been through this so many times before, but still, she was always taken by surprise, even though she tried to be on guard with him. "I don't baby them, Robert. I only want the best for them…Bobby, too. Why don't you sit down, talk to the girls, and really get to know them? We could be a real family. That's all they've ever wanted."

His eyes narrowed. "You'll always take their side against me." He shook his head slowly back and forth. "It never fails. To be perfectly honest, they get on my nerves. Especially Frankie and that damned music of hers. Thump, thump, thump, that's all I ever hear. That stereo is going in the rubbish! That crap she listens to is warping her mind!"

Anger flashed in Farrel's eyes. "That stereo was a gift from her grandmother. It's going to stay in her room. Besides, there's nothing wrong with music. I love listening to it, too."

"What did you say?" he asked as his eyes bore into hers. "Did I just hear you question my authority again? Have you forgotten *who* the head of this family is?" he shouted. "You exasperate me, Farrel."

Farrel's bottom lip trembled. She prepared herself for what was surely to come next.

"Answer me!"

Before she could utter a sound, Robert shoved her. "You are pushing me to the limit," he snarled. "I won't tolerate any more of your disrespect for my authority!" He slapped her across the mouth with the back of his hand.

Blood spurted from her lip. His eyes were wild as he came at her with raised fists. "No!" she screamed, trying to cover her face. "I'm sorry! I won't question your authority again," she pleaded as she backed away from him. "Please don't hit me. Stop it, Robert!"

"You should have thought about that!" He pressed her against the wall, pinning her with one muscular arm as the fist of his other arm came crashing down on her chin. "Is this the way you like to be treated, whore? Like the women you write about?"

Farrel fell to the floor in a heap. The pain that tore through her was worse than anything she had ever felt before. The beating from Robert proved that his violence toward her was escalating.

Robert was instantly at her side. He bent down to look at her and then knelt down to where she lay. He picked her head up, laid it in his lap, and began to stroke her hair. "Baby, what's wrong with you? Don't you know how much I love you?" Tears slid down his cheeks. "I would never hurt you. I'm only trying to protect you from yourself."

Charly strolled into the kitchen. "What's going on?" she asked as she flipped her auburn hair over her shoulder. "Why are you guys on the floor?" she asked with a laugh in her voice as she walked closer, and then suddenly stopped. Her eyed widened. "Mom?" She stood above her mother and stared down at her. "Mom, what happened?" she asked as she looked in horror at her mother's bruised and bloodied face.

"I'm okay, honey. I just had a little accident," Farrel whispered through clenched teeth. "I'll be fine. Give me a minute," she said, pausing after every word.

"This isn't a *little accident*, Mom." Charly whirled on her stepfather. "You hit her again, didn't you?" she demanded.

"I have *never* hit your mother!" Robert's face flushed angrily. "I resent your accusation!"

Charly's eyes filled with tears as she looked at him in disbelief. "How can you lie about it? You beat her all the time." She turned back to her mother. "Why don't we leave, Mom? Let's go tonight."

"Honey, I'll be fine," Farrel whispered as she took her daughter's delicate hand and slowly rose to her feet. She gave her a long hug, sucking in her breath as her body throbbed with excruciating pain. "Why don't you take a hot shower and get to bed early? You look tired."

"Mom, your face. He hit you, admit it," she cried. "I'm going to call the police!"

"Don't you threaten me!" Robert grabbed her arm. "This is not a police matter. Your mother had an accident, that's all."

"Don't touch me!" Charly's eyes flashed as she slapped his hand off her arm. "You're sick!" she spat at him before stomping out of the room.

Robert turned back to Farrel. "You should feel so proud to have brought two ungrateful brats like your daughters into this world! They are a mockery to God and everything He stands for."

"Robert, they are my children, and I love them very much. I'm sorry that you're jealous of them, but I will not have them living this way any longer. I can't take it anymore. Do you hear me?" Tears streamed down her face. "I've tried to make this marriage work, Robert. I wanted my girls to have a normal happy family experience." Anger overtook her pain. "You need to take a good hard look at yourself. If you're truthful, then you will see that you are *not* a good father. You're not a good person."

"What do you mean by that?" he demanded, his face turning an ugly shade of purple.

"Look what you've done to your son. The way you've raised him, I fear for his future relationships with women. I don't want any woman to put up with what I have from him."

"Don't you dare say a word about Bobby. He's a good boy," he stated. "You've always been jealous of him."

Farrel sighed heavily. "It's useless to talk to you. Everything is so one-sided with you, and it always will be!" She put her hand to her chin. "Why, Robert? Why do you hurt me? Does it make you feel like a man? Does it make you feel powerful to beat and berate me? Do you think God justifies what you're doing?" She paused. "I can't live this way anymore."

"And where would you go?" Robert smirked. "Your mouth is going to get you into serious trouble someday. I give you a good life, and this is what I get in return." He shrugged. "I don't know what you expect from a husband. Maybe that's why your first one left you. Get yourself into the bathroom before Frankie gets home and accuses me of beating you."

Farrel looked in disbelief at him as she laid a hand on his arm. "Robert, they see what you're doing. They aren't blind. They see my bruises. How can you deny it?" Her lips trembled. "You can get help. You don't have to be this way."

"Don't touch me!" His voice was icy. "You don't know my needs," he sneered. "And even if you did, you wouldn't be capable of fulfilling them."

"I'm your wife! I don't deserve this treatment." She blinked hard. "How would you feel if some man treated your mother the way you treat me?"

He rolled his eyes. "Don't bring my mother into this. She's a good woman, and would give no one any cause to harm her."

"You'd never tolerate her being verbally and physically abused."

"Just leave me alone! You push me too far, Farrel. I don't know why I ever married you. That's one time I wish I would have listened to my mother." His eyes slanted. "She's never steered me wrong. You're just upset because she sees right through you to the ugly blackness of your soul. I've treated you better than anyone you've ever known."

"No, you haven't! You started out emotionally abusing me." She looked into his eyes. "But when you found out that you were illegitimate, you started physically abusing me. It's been eating you alive. You need to talk to your mother about it…bring it out into the open. Ask her why she never told you, and especially find out who your real father is."

"Don't you ever talk about my mother!" he shouted. His facial muscles twitched uncontrollably, and his breath came in heavy spurts. He roughly gripped her arm and then twisted it.

"Let go, Robert!" she screamed. "You're going to break my arm!" She squeezed her eyes shut as a sharp jolt tore through her shoulder. His grip felt like a vise had been clamped on her arm as he kept twisting it.

"I want you to feel the same intense suffering you've caused me to feel," he said as he shoved her until her back was wedged against the counter.

"I don't know what you're talking about. Please let me go," she pleaded. If he pushed any harder, her arm was going to snap. Tears streamed down her face. She was going to pass out if he didn't stop.

"I warned you, but you never listen," he whispered menacingly. "No one ever listens to me. Maybe now you'll realize who's the boss around here. I know what's good for you."

Farrel looked into his eyes. They were devoid of any emotion, only staring back at her, vacant, and lost. "Please, Robert," she pleaded again. "I know you don't really want to hurt me." She gasped as he tugged her arm more forcefully. Fresh tears squeezed out of her tightly closed eyes. "No!" she shrieked as a sickening blackness almost overtook her. "Charly!"

"Can't you hear the shower, Farrel? She can't hear you. And if Frankie was home, she'd have that evil music blaring. No one can hear you," he whispered in her ear. "Not one soul. It's just you and me."

"The neighbors...they'll know something's wrong."

"The neighbors don't care about you. They don't hear me yelling. They probably wish I would shut you the hell up."

"Please, Robert," she cried. She hoped Betty Levitt would hear her. But if the police came, would Farrel be brave enough to tell them the truth? Robert was right...she had nowhere to go and no one to turn to. But she had to do something—if not for herself, then for her daughters' sakes.

He ignored her. "You have so much evil inside of you, Farrel." His voice was firm. "It is my Godly duty as your husband to release this evil from within you."

"Robert, I am not evil. I'm a good person."

"No." He looked into her eyes. "You can't see the evil within you. I can see it, though."

"You are the one who's evil," she said in a raspy voice. "The things you do to me are from a sick mind. You have no right to hurt me."

His eyes narrowed until they were two dark slits. "How dare you accuse me of abuse?!"

He tightened his grip and twisted her arm with all the strength he possessed. She screamed as her bone separated from her shoulder.

Robert let go of her arm and frowned as he looked at her. "You'll be all right. Get up."

"Robert," Farrel whispered hoarsely. Tears rolled down her cheeks. "I'm not all right. You've got to help me!"

Frankie burst into the room with Bobby at her heels. "Mom!" she screamed as she rushed to her mother's side, kneeling down beside her. "What happened?"

"She tripped over something on the floor," Robert said.

Bobby laughed. "You'd better watch where you're going, Farrel." He turned to his father. "Dad, I've got a game on Sunday—two o'clock at Whipple Field." His eyes flashed excitedly. "The coach said I'm the most improved player of the week!"

Robert heartily slapped his son on the back. "I knew you could do it, Bobby."

Frankie's eyes widened. "I can't believe you two. How

can you stand there talking about baseball when Mom is lying on the floor in pain? I'm calling an ambulance."

"No. Your mother is fine." He looked at his wife. "Tell her, Farrel," he said with a noticeable warning in his voice.

Farrel glared at him. "No, I'm not fine. I think my arm is broken." Her voice cracked.

"Oh, Mom!" Frankie cried.

"She'll be all right," Robert said again. "I'll put her to bed, and she'll be fine in the morning."

"No!" Farrel screamed. "I need to get to a hospital!"

Charly ran into the room. "What's all the yelling about? Another fight?"

"Robert broke Mom's arm," Frankie stated as she glared at her stepfather with hate filled eyes.

"Oh, right," Bobby said sarcastically. "My dad never touched your mother."

"You weren't here," Frankie shot back.

"Neither were you," Bobby replied.

"She's going to the hospital," Frankie insisted.

"And just what are you going to tell them at the hospital?" Robert asked, looking intently at Farrel. "How will you explain all of your bruises?"

"I don't know, Robert!" she shrieked. "I'm in too much pain to think straight. Just help me!"

"Tell them the truth, Mom, that Robert did it," Charly said. "Tell them that he's been doing it forever."

"My dad never touched Farrel, you liar!" Bobby yelled.

"You know that he beats Mom all the time. You're the liar. You're just afraid to admit it because you're afraid of your father. But then everybody knows you're afraid of your own shadow, wimp!" Charly yelled back.

"Don't you ever call my son a liar!" Robert's voice boomed

as he grabbed Charly and slammed her against the wall.

"Get your hands off my sister!" Frankie cried. She pulled on Robert's arm.

"I've been good to you two. You are nothing but ingrates. My son has sacrificed so much for the both of you."

"No, he hasn't!" Frankie yelled. "He's always had everything handed to him. There's always enough money to get him what he wants, while Charly and I have to do without!"

Robert raised his fist.

"Don't you dare, Robert!" Farrel screamed. "So help me, as God is my witness, I'll have you locked up for the rest of your life."

He lowered his fist as he released Charly, then turned to face his wife. "Don't you ever threaten me!" He walked over to her and squatted until he was eye level with her.

Perspiration trickled down Farrel's face. "Please get me some help now, Robert." She didn't know how much longer she could hold on.

He grinned at her. "You need help for your mental problems. I should have you committed, Farrel. You're always imagining things," he taunted.

"Whatever you say, Robert." She sucked in her breath as she turned her face away from his sickening grin.

"Help her, Robert!" Frankie screamed. "I'm calling an ambulance."

"No. I'll drive her to the hospital. Now get off my damned back!" He looked threateningly at Farrel. "You'd better be careful what you tell them at the hospital."

<<<>>>

Twenty minutes later, Farrel sat on a chair in a little cubicle in the emergency room.

"They've got a head-on collision with multiple injuries," Robert said as he entered the cubicle. "It's going to be quite a long wait." He shoved his hands into his pockets. "At least your arm is taken care of. I don't know why we have to wait."

"They want to run some tests." Farrel eyed herself in her compact mirror. The harsh, bright light glared down on her. With her good arm, she patted powder on her swollen and bruised face. She knew that she had once been not so bad looking. She was never what you would call a beauty, but she had always been considered cute. But her looks were now hidden behind this mask of hideous contusions.

"You know what to say." Robert stared at her. "The same thing you said when they set your arm."

Farrel looked up. "Yes, Robert," she answered tiredly. She tried to shift to a more comfortable position, but with every movement she made, she winced in pain. She had to take her mind off her present agony, or she would never bear it for however long she had to wait for the tests. The pain pill they'd given her hadn't fully kicked in yet. She wasn't in the mood to make small talk with Robert. Especially to put on the phony act that they were a loving couple.

Farrel sighed. Her life was a lie—her whole adult life had been a lie. She wondered why happiness always seemed to elude her—or worse yet, why she chose men who promised to love her forever, but in the end, only hurt her. Farrel closed her eyes and recalled the day she'd met Ben Stuart, her first husband—the father of her children. That seemed like a lifetime ago now.

<<<>>>

Farrel sat quietly, watching a volleyball game. She didn't notice the tall stranger approaching until he was beside her.

"Mind if I sit down?" he asked.

She gave him a sideways glance. "No."

"Why aren't you out there with them?" he asked.

She turned her head slightly and couldn't help but notice how physically attractive he was. "I'm not in the mood," she curtly answered, wishing he would go away and leave her alone.

He sat down next to her. "I'm not much of a volleyball player myself," he said as he picked at the grass. "So, who are you here with?"

"My sister." Farrel pointed to an attractive, sunburned blonde in the first row.

"Oh, Cheryl. I'm her boss."

"I know."

He lifted a surprised eyebrow. "Do you have a first name?" he asked.

"Farrel."

"Farrel Thorpe. Glad to meet you. I'm—"

"I already know. Ben Stuart." Her voice held no emotion.

"You seem upset. Is something bothering you?" His tone was friendly.

"No."

"You could have fooled me."

She sighed. "See that guy over there?"

Ben followed the direction of her extended finger. "You mean the guy in the black trunks who's falling all over the redhead?"

"That's him."

"So?"

Farrel frowned. "He's supposed to be with me."

"So why do you put up with it?" he asked gently.

"There isn't exactly an overabundance of men around this town."

Ben smiled. "By the looks of you, you should have no trouble finding a decent guy."

She smiled too. "Maybe I don't look in the right places. Maybe I should start looking outside of town."

That was the beginning of what she thought would be the happiest time of her life. Ben Stuart literally swept her off her feet. After a whirlwind courtship, they moved to Connecticut, bought a house, and settled into a happy routine as newlyweds.

Ben treated her like a queen, and there was nothing she wouldn't do for him. As CEO of a large company, he was often away on long business trips for weeks at a time. Farrel kept busy taking care of the house, planting a large vegetable garden, and writing. She had felt odd telling Ben about her writing ambitions, and thought he would laugh it off as everyone else had, but instead, he was impressed and encouraged her. At the age of twenty-one, she had her life mapped out.

But in one short minute, Farrel's world fell apart and came crashing down around her. She was six months pregnant with Frankie when, while cleaning Ben's desk one day, she came across a letter from a woman named Loren Stuart. The letter was intimate, and she knew she shouldn't have read it. Ben had warned her not to ever go near his desk, but it was such a mess that she wanted to surprise him. Farrel never expected that she would be the one to be surprised. Her hand trembled, her chest tightened, and her head grew light as she held the letter. She sat down at the kitchen table, still holding the letter in her hand as hot tears rolled down her cheeks. She squeezed her eyes tightly shut, but her tears pounded against her lids. Like a burst dam, the tears trickled out of her eyes. She popped her eyes open, and they once again poured down her cheeks, sweeping away her perfect life and washing away all of her dreams.

That was how Ben found her when he returned home that evening. "What's wrong, honey?" he anxiously asked as he looked at her red, swollen eyes and tearstained cheeks. "Is it the baby? Has something happened to the baby?"

She thrust the letter at him. "I found this," she choked out.

"What's this?" He glanced at the letter. "Oh, God!" His face grew white. "It's not what you think—let me explain." He laid a hand on her shoulder.

She shrugged him off. "I think the letter is self-explanatory," she sniffed. She removed her wedding ring and laid it on the table. Tears glistened in her eyes.

"Farrel...honey, let's talk about it. Let me explain."

"There's nothing to explain. We're not married, Ben. These past two years have been a lie. And what's worse, you're a bigamist."

He shook his head. "No, you don't understand. Al wasn't a real justice of the peace."

Farrel felt as though an arrow had just pierced her heart. "I don't believe it! You were married to someone else, then had a phony marriage to me?" She looked incredulously at him. "And you think this makes everything better?"

"Honey, I didn't want to lose you." His eyes filled with tears. "I couldn't stand it if you left me."

"Get off it, Ben. You were cheating on your wife!" She looked down at her stomach and gently patted it. "You know the funny part?" she asked as she raised her eyes and looked into his. "I really thought you were different—someone I could believe in who wouldn't lie to me. But you're no different."

"Listen to me for just a minute," he pleaded. "Loren and I

were finished before I ever met you. We just hadn't legalized it. I never intended to get married again, so I didn't bother filing for a divorce." He lamely added the last part. "And Loren felt the same way."

"Then why weren't you honest with me?" She stared at him. "You know how I cannot stand being lied to. How can I ever trust you again?"

Ben grabbed her hand. "Honey, please listen. I loved you from the moment I laid eyes on you. If you knew I was married, you never would have gone out with me. I told you, I couldn't bear to lose you."

"You're right that I would have never gone out with you if I'd known your marital status."

"What choice did I have? It wasn't like Loren and I were living together or sharing the same bed."

"What about the baby? Were you just going to let us have a phony marriage forever?" Farrel asked the questions one after the other without giving him a chance to answer.

"I love you, Farrel, and I love our baby you're carrying." He affectionately patted her stomach. "I can't say I'm sorry enough, but you have to believe how much I love you. I'll call a lawyer and get a divorce from Loren, and then we can be married legally. No one has to know." His eyes pleaded with her. "Please?"

"For the baby's sake, I see no other way," she quietly answered. "Do you think the divorce will take long?"

"It shouldn't." His eyes brightened. "We'll get through this, Farrel."

"I want things to be right before the baby is born. I want our child to be born to us as husband and wife."

"I promise."

But it was a promise Ben could not keep, even though

he did everything in his power not to break his word to her. Frankie Lynn Stuart came into the world four months before they could legally be married.

Farrel busied herself in her new role as mother and rarely thought about Ben's deception. Soon they settled into a cozy routine and were once again a happy couple.

A little over two years later, they were once again blessed with a child. Charly Jane Stuart arrived early, barely giving them time to prepare for her entrance into the world. But they excitedly welcomed her with the same love as they had Frankie.

During Farrel's pregnancy with Charly, she hadn't been aware of Ben's withdrawal from her. It happened so subtly that she couldn't even remember when it had really begun. Her days and nights had been filled with taking care of Frankie, a very active toddler. By the time she fell into bed at night, Ben was usually fast asleep, or he was at work until the wee hours of the morning. Because it had been weeks since she had been able to have sex, Ben's distancing from her had gone unnoticed until she had her six-week check-up. She remembered that night so well.

It was a Friday night, so she knew that Ben wouldn't have to go into work the next morning unless he wanted to. And she knew that he wouldn't want to after the night she had planned for him. Charly was sleeping through the night now, and Farrel knew that by giving Frankie an early nap, she would be sound asleep by eight o'clock.

Farrel had prepared an intimate dinner for two in front of the fireplace, and set candles on the hearth as well as the table. She showered and then slipped into a form-hugging black dress that had always been a favorite of Ben's. It clung to her in all the right places. There was no way Ben would be able to hold back all of his pent-up sexual frustration that he must have been feeling these past few weeks. Farrel had worked hard exercising to get her body back to her pre-childbirth days, and her hard work had paid off as she looked at her sleek, slender form in the full-length closet mirror. In fact, she felt better than she ever had in her entire life. She was firm and well-toned.

Ben had called and told her that he would be late, and almost ruined her surprise when he said he would grab a bite to eat downtown. Farrel had assured him that she wouldn't mind having a late dinner with him. He arrived home about nine p.m. She met him at the door, and before he had a chance to utter a word, led him silently into the living room. He smiled sheepishly at the table and then held her away from him for a moment as his eyes rested on her.

"Do you like what you see?" she asked expectantly.

He smiled. "I love what I see. I'm starved."

Farrel was disappointed that he hadn't immediately swept her into his arms. It wasn't until dinner was over, and she led him to the bedroom that she discovered the reason for his reluctance. She lay seductively on the bed, enticing him with her eyes. When she got no response, she knew that something was deeply troubling him. "What's wrong, Ben?" she finally asked. "Are you having problems at work?"

"No. It's not work." He stuffed his hands into his pockets and turned towards the window. "I know you wanted tonight to be special, Farrel." His voice was tinged with guilt and sadness.

"Please, Ben," her voice shook. "Just tell me what's going on." She tried to steady her voice.

Ben sighed deeply and then turned to face her. She could see the tears in his eyes, and it frightened her.

"I want out."

Ben said it abruptly and in a low voice, barely audible above her thundering heartbeat. Her ears pounded with every beat of her heart. Farrel must have misunderstood him. They had everything going for them. All of their hopes and dreams were now coming true. She was sure that she had misunderstood him. He meant something else, not the demise of their life together. "I don't understand," she numbly said.

He walked over to the bed and sat on the edge, then gently took her hand in his. "I never wanted to hurt you or the kids. You're a great wife and mother."

"But?" she asked as her eyes filled with tears.

"Please believe me when I say I don't want to hurt you, Farrel. That was never my intention." His voice pleaded for her understanding.

Farrel's lips quivered as she fought for composure. "Is there someone else?" She stared into his eyes, but in her heart, she already knew the answer.

"I don't even know how it happened." A tear slid from his eye.

She had never seen him cry before. "Are you asking me for a divorce, Ben?"

Ben squeezed his eyes tightly shut, as though his answer were too painful to allow him to look into her eyes. "Yes," he choked.

A tremor began in Farrel's heart and slowly spread throughout her body. She had so many questions that needed to be answered, but could not get her brain to send the message to her lips.

"I'm so sorry, Farrel." He dropped her hand. "I'll be moving my things out in a few days. But for now, I'll stay in the guest room."

Numb, she nodded.

<<<>>>

"Sorry for the delay. I'm Dr. Fellows."

The deep friendly voice jolted Farrel back to the present. She blinked her eyes as though she had just awoken from a deep sleep.

Robert stood up. "My wife fell in our apartment and banged herself up pretty badly. Her arm is broken and has been taken care of, but we were told some tests needed to be performed before she can be released."

The doctor looked at Farrel. "That's right. The tests might take a little while. Someone will come to get you in a few minutes." Dr. Fellows turned to Robert. "We have a waiting room if you'd prefer to wait there while the tests are being performed."

"Is that necessary?" he asked. "Can't I wait here?"

"If you prefer," the doctor replied. "I just thought you might be more comfortable in the waiting room."

Robert shifted uneasily and then shot Farrel a warning look. "All right. I'll go get a cup of coffee."

Dr. Fellows turned his attention back to Farrel after Robert left. He frowned. "Why don't you tell me what really happened?" he asked softly.

Farrel was surprised at his question. "It's like my husband said. I slipped on the kitchen floor and smashed my face into a cabinet. My arm must have broken when I fell."

The doctor sighed as he continued to stare at her. He checked her vital statistics. "You have a broken arm, but I'm more concerned about what's broken on the inside."

He didn't believe her, and she wished she could tell him the truth, but Robert's wrath would be worse than she could ever imagine if she told the doctor what Robert had done to her. She offered the doctor a weak smile. "I'm just accident prone. That's all."

"Uh-huh," he answered. He gently touched the bruises on her face. "You have new contusions over old ones."

Farrel's face reddened, but she didn't answer him even though he seemed to expect an answer.

"After your tests, I'm going to have someone talk to you."

"Why?"

"Because I see too much of this battering in here every night. Maybe I can help one woman get out of the cycle."

Farrel looked into his soft gray eyes and saw his compassion. "I'll be okay. I'm just clumsy."

"I just hope I'm not on duty when your next visit here is to the morgue."

CHAPTER THREE

"Hi, Farrel...may I call you Farrel?" a friendly voice questioned as she held out a hand in greeting.

Farrel nodded, looking quizzically at the pretty older woman.

"My name is Mary, and I'm a volunteer at the Domestic Violence Center."

"There must be a mistake," Farrel answered quickly. "I'm waiting for someone to take me for some tests." She paused. "My husband and I don't have any problems."

"I see," the woman answered as her eyes gave Farrel the once-over. "You know that no one has the right to hurt you." Her voice was soft and motherly. "I was in your situation many years ago, Farrel. That was before we had somewhere to go for help. In my generation, a woman was supposed to take her husband's abuse. We had no options back then, but some of us went against the norm and filed for divorce... others weren't so lucky. You have a choice today...a choice that I wish I would have had."

Farrel dropped her eyes from Mary's, which seemed to peer into her soul, right to all the secret places no one could ever know about. "There must be a mistake. Robert has never hurt me." She glanced at her cast-encased arm. "I'm clumsy, that's all."

Mary sighed. "Okay, I don't want to press you."

Farrel wondered if Mary picked up on her fear. If she had once been in Farrel's shoes, then she must certainly know that Robert would deny any wrongdoing, and her life would become even more unbearable than it was now if she told anyone.

Mary dug a card out of her pocket. "If you ever need to talk to someone, Jerry Feldon is a great guy. He's helped me through many rough times. And you can always call me if you ever want to talk." She smiled.

Farrel reluctantly took the card, knowing she'd never use it. "Thank you, but I really don't think I'll be needing it."

Mary patted her shoulder. "Just in case," she said softly. "Just in case." She pulled up a stool and seated herself. "I'd like to sit with you while you wait if that's okay."

Farrel shrugged. "I don't mind." She sensed that Mary was hoping she would spill her guts, but Mary surprised her and chatted about her children, grandchildren, and her varied interests. Farrel envied the woman. Mary had a full vibrant life, quite the contrast to her situation years earlier, which she'd described in vibrant detail.

Mary went with her when Farrel was whisked away for her tests, and then accompanied her back to the examination room. Farrel was grateful for Mary's help in getting dressed. Mary continued to wait with her until the doctor came to give Farrel her discharge papers and instructions.

<<<>>>

Robert was waiting for her outside the examination room.

"Who was that woman?" he asked. "The doctor told me you were getting dressed. I didn't know you were talking to anyone else."

Farrel slipped the card and the prescription the doctor had

given her for painkillers into her pocket. "She was helping me to get dressed."

Robert's eyes narrowed. "What did you tell her?"

"Nothing. I told you she was only there to help me get dressed. That's all," she lied.

"Good...good. Let's get out of here." He gently took her elbow and led her to the exit. "By the way, what was that you stuffed into your pocket?"

"A prescription for pain killers," she answered.

"Okay. We'll pick it up on the way home."

<<<>>>

Robert gently unbuttoned Farrel's blouse and then helped her out of it. "The kids sure got a kick out of decorating the cast."

"Yeah, they put some strange things on here. Especially Frankie with her artistic flare." Farrel sat on the edge of the bed so Robert could pull her pants off. She thought about how gentle and loving he had been all the way home. He had even been warm and kind to the girls. But would his good mood last? Could it last? She frowned. His mood swings frightened her. But maybe this time he realized he'd gone too far. Maybe he *would* change. She had to hold on to that hope.

"Climb into bed, honey. I've got a couple of pillows to prop your arm on."

Farrel bit her bottom lip as her arm began to throb again. She was exhausted, but she knew that sleep would never come unless she took another pain killer. As opposed as she was to mind-altering drugs, the pain was too intense to ignore. "Robert, could you get me a pain pill, please?" she asked.

"Of course. I'm going to take good care of you, Farrel. I promise." He brought her a glass of water and a pill.

After she swallowed the pill and took a drink of water,

he took the glass from her and set it on the bedside table. Farrel watched him as he slipped off his clothes and climbed into bed beside her, being careful not to disturb her arm. He dimmed the lamp. It cast a soft glow over the room.

Farrel turned her head and faced him. "Robert, can we talk?" Her voice was low.

"Sure, what's on your mind?" He tenderly ran his fingertips across her cheek.

Farrel took a deep breath. "Robert, are you sorry that you married me?"

"Of course not. Why would you ever think that?" He turned and looked at her. "I loved you from the moment I first laid eyes on you." He gently brushed his lips against hers. "I couldn't imagine life without you. You'll never know how much I love you and need you in my life."

Farrel blinked back the tears threatening to fall. "Then why, Robert, if you love me so much, do you always hurt me?"

"I could never hurt you, Farrel. And I would never let anyone else ever hurt you," he said tenderly. "I think those pills are clouding your mind."

Farrel couldn't believe her ears. How could he deny what he had done? She wondered if he really didn't know what he was doing. He was as different as day and night. When he was bad, he was violent, but when he was good, he was the sweetest man alive. If only he could reach a happy medium. His levels were either high or low; he was never on an even plateau. It wasn't normal, and he would never admit any wrongdoing on his part.

She touched her cast. How could Robert not know what he had done to her only a few hours earlier? He had to know that he'd broken her arm. There was no way he could deny his physical abuse. How could he beat her one minute and then be tender and loving the next as though nothing had happened? Had Robert somehow managed to block his actions from his mind? It was twisted. If he really didn't believe he'd done anything wrong, then he was very disturbed. And if he knew he did it but thought his actions were justified, that also was the product of a deeply disturbed mind.

"What are you thinking about, honey?" Robert asked softly as he sifted her hair through his fingers.

"Robert, I love you so much," she whispered.

"I love you too, Farrel." He ran the back of his hand over her cheek. "What's bothering you?"

She drew a deep breath and then slowly exhaled. "We need to get our lives on track. All of this fighting isn't good for the kids."

"The kids are fine. They know that parents have arguments. No one gets along all of the time. A little friction now and then is good for them. They can't go into the world expecting perfection."

"There's a difference, Robert. What they see you do to me is not normal. I don't want the girls to think any man has the right to abuse them. And I certainly don't want Bobby to think that he has the right to abuse any woman." Farrel gazed at her husband and watched his facial muscles begin to twitch. She didn't know what to expect next. He was obviously struggling to keep himself under control.

Robert leaned forward and kissed her forehead. "Look, it's been a long day. Let's get some sleep." His voice was still soft.

"Robert?"

He sighed tiredly. "What, Farrel?"

"Would you consider marriage counseling?"

He was silent for a moment before answering. "If it would make you happy. But I personally think it's a waste of time and money. No one really benefits from it. The past gets dragged up, and then it only makes the situation worse. It's better to let sleeping dogs lie. People need to work their problems out on their own."

"But would you go, Robert?" she persisted.

He propped himself up on an elbow and gazed down at her. "Yes, Farrel. If that's what you want."

"Thank you. It's a start...a positive start."

<<<>>>

"Charly...Charly Stuart!"

Charly jumped. "Sorry, Miss Wymer. I didn't hear the question."

The class burst into laughter as Charly's face reddened. She had no idea what Miss Wymer had asked her. Her mind had drifted far away. Away to a place that was happy and secure. Far away from her home.

Karla Miller poked her in the back. "Way to go, Charly," she snickered. "It's about time you got knocked off your goody-two-shoes pedestal."

"I asked you if you finished your math assignment last night. Please come to the board and write down the equation," the teacher said sharply. "We have a lot of work to cover before finals."

Charly quickly shuffled through her folder. "Yeah, it's here somewhere." She continued searching for the missing assignment.

"You don't have it, do you, Charly?" Miss Wymer asked.

"Yeah, I think I do. I thought I did it." She tossed her head. "I know it's here somewhere." She flipped through her math book.

"Charly, I don't have time for these games. Either you have your assignment, or you don't. Which is it?"

"Give me a break," Charly muttered under her breath.

"You know the rules. No homework, then detention until the assignment is completed. I'll see you after school."

"I can't, Miss Wymer," she pleaded.

Karla snickered. "Join the crowd, Charly. It's not so bad."

Charly turned around in her seat and faced Karla. "Just shut up, Karla!"

"That's enough!" Miss Wymer shouted. "Charly Stuart, go to the principal's office immediately!"

Charly turned back around, red-faced and embarrassed. "But Miss Wymer —" she protested.

"Now!" the teacher ordered.

Karla snickered.

"Karla Miller, if you'd like to join her, you may. Otherwise, keep your mouth closed."

Karla bit her bottom lip to suppress her laughter. "Yes, Miss Wymer."

Charly grabbed her books. "I think you're being unfair, Miss Wymer."

"We'll discuss it later, Charly. But not on my class time!"

<<<>>>

"I got you a cola, Frankie," Gary Blackmon said as he set the drink on Frankie's lunch tray.

"Thanks."

"Want to see a movie tonight?" he asked.

"I don't know." She blew her breath out and frowned. "I'd like to, but I don't think I should leave my mom right now."

Gary touched her shoulder. "What's wrong with your mother? Is she sick?"

Frankie stared down at her uneaten lunch. "No. It's worse."

Gary's eyes narrowed. "Did your step-dad do something again?" he persisted.

She looked into her boyfriend's caring eyes. She swallowed hard. "Yes, he broke her arm last night."

"That bastard." Gary protectively put an arm around Frankie's shoulder. "He didn't do anything to you, did he? I swear, if he did—"

She shook her head. "No. But I think he would have hit me if my mom hadn't stopped him." Tears filled her eyes. "Gary, I can't take it anymore. We don't live in a home—we live in a war-zone. It keeps getting worse, and I don't know how much more I can take." She bit down on her trembling lip.

He grunted. "He'd better not lay a hand on you, Frankie. I mean it. I just wish there was something I could do."

Frankie peered into his eyes. "I don't know why you even put up with me when you could date any girl in this school. You don't need all of this constant drama."

"I don't want any other girl. I only want you." He squeezed her hand. "How about if I come over after baseball practice, and if you don't feel like going to a movie, we can watch some TV at your place."

Frankie smiled. "Okay, but I can't promise what the home front will be like."

"I'll take my chances. Just so I get to spend time with you." He smiled.

The bell rang, sending everyone scurrying to empty lunch trays and gather books for the next class.

"I've got to get to math," Frankie said, rolling her eyes.

"I'll take your tray. I've got Phys ed. I'll see you after

school."

<<<>>>

Charly caught Frankie's arm as Frankie was rummaging through her locker.

"What's up?" Frankie asked as she grabbed a stack of books.

"I got in trouble in math class, and Wymer sent me to the principal. I got a week's detention." She shrugged her shoulders. "I don't know how to tell Mom."

"Yeah, she certainly doesn't need this after everything she's been through." She shot a sharp look at her younger sister.

"What do you want from me, Frankie—blood? It was just one of those things. I couldn't help it."

"Well, maybe you should try growing up! I suppose Karla was involved."

Charly rolled her eyes. "Why do you always pick on her? I don't do that to your friends."

"Because Karla is a bad influence on you. Face it, Charly, Karla is a loser. She's such an airhead that if anyone pricked her head, she would go floating off into Never Never Land. She couldn't care less about anything except having a good time."

"Frankie, get off my case! Your head is always in the clouds over *Gary the Geek*. You don't live in the real world. Face reality! Our life stinks! Ever since Mom married Robert, we've gone downhill. We certainly aren't the close, loving family Robert pretends we are."

Frankie held a hand palm up. "Okay, calm down. I'll handle Mom, but don't you ever call Gary a geek again. You don't even know him. If you did, you would see what a great guy he is. He's definitely not like that loser Mike Williams you were gawking after. The *Acne King*."

"Come on, Mike wasn't that bad. He just has problems."

"Whatever. Look, I've got to get to class. Try to stay out of trouble for the rest of the day."

"Thanks for covering with Mom for me. I owe you one, Sis. Gotta go. I can't afford to be late for history."

Farrel slowly opened the door and quickly composed herself as she greeted her neighbor. "Hello, Betty."

"Good morning, Farrel. I was just on my way outside and thought I'd stop to see if you'd like to visit with me for a while."

"I'd love to, but I'm not feeling well today." She nodded to her arm. "I broke my arm last night."

"Oh, dear, do you need any help? Is there anything I can do for you?"

Farrel shook her head. "I'll be fine. Thanks."

"How did it happen?" Betty asked as her eyes swept past Farrel and took in the immaculate living room. As much as she would have enjoyed Farrel's company, she knew that her true reason for stopping was to be certain that Farrel was all right after the commotion last night. If it hadn't been for Bill, Betty would have come to Farrel's aid, or at the very least called the police, but Bill had said to mind her own business and let the Drakes work out their own problems. Her heart went out to Farrel. Everyone she had talked to this morning knew about the Drakes' latest battle. Their fights were becoming legendary throughout the building.

"I slipped in the kitchen last night. It was one of those things." Farrel laughed weakly.

"Well, if you need anything at all, please don't hesitate to ask."

"Thank you, Betty, but Robert has been a big help to me."

<<<>>>

Farrel closed the door, and then slowly let her breath out. She knew that Betty Levitt hadn't believed her. There was no way that anyone could look at her and not know that she'd been severely beaten. She walked over to the sofa and sat down. Farrel was relieved that Robert had kept his loving demeanor all through breakfast. Even the kids seemed surprised by his attitude. No one had even mentioned the events of the previous night. All five of them sat around the kitchen table, eating breakfast and chatting like any normal family. But underneath it all, there had been tension—a thick, nerve-wrenching tension she'd feared would snap at any moment. But it hadn't. Robert had remained sweet and tender. He'd helped her dress and had even made breakfast for his family. She smiled. Maybe there was hope after all. Maybe she and Robert could get along, and she could show the girls what a normal family was really like. They might even feel loved and wanted...Farrel and her daughters. Robert would finally show them that he did care about them. He would change. He *had* to change. She had to cling to that hope. She needed something to hold on to. She could forgive him for everything in the past if she had a normal future to hold on to. "Please, God, let him stay this way. Let him be the husband I know he can be."

<<<>>>

Karla caught Charly's arm as Charly rushed toward the gym. "What's your hurry?" she asked.

"I don't want to be late, Karla. You've gotten me in enough trouble today." Her tone was cool.

"Lighten up, Charly. You know, you're becoming a real drag lately." She narrowed her eyes as she scrutinized her friend. "What's going on with you anyway?"

"Nothing, Karla. Just the same old stuff. Look, I really have to go."

"Want to do something tonight?"

"I doubt I'll be going anywhere. I'm probably going to be grounded for the rest of my life," she said disgustedly.

"Well, you can't blame me. Wymer lost it when you were off in La La Land." She grabbed Charly's arm. "So tell me what's really up. I'm supposed to be your best friend, remember?"

Charly shrugged. "Nothing. I'm just sick and tired of Robert. I can't stand to see my mother knocked around."

"So, what's the evil one done now?"

Charly's eyes filled with tears. "He beat the crap out of my mother last night and broke her arm."

"Oh, wow! I'm sorry, Charly." She patted Charly's arm. "Why don't you talk to someone about it? Mrs. Browning handles stuff like that."

"No. Robert would have a fit if he found out. I've just got to convince my mom to leave him."

"Hey, I'll come over tonight, okay? If the evil one puts too much pressure on you, I'll tell him it's my fault you got detention."

"Thanks, Karla. Well, I really gotta go. I'll see you tonight."

<<<>>>

Robert set his briefcase on the kitchen counter. "How was your day, Farrel?" His voice was soft.

"Quiet." She smiled. "How was yours?"

"The usual," he replied. "How's the arm?"

"As long as I take my pain pills, it's not too bad. I couldn't do too much around here with one arm, so I caught up on some reading."

51

He nodded. "Where are the kids?"

She nervously cleared her throat. "Robert, we have to talk."

"I don't know if I like the sound of that." His eyes narrowed as he pulled out a chair and sat down. "What's wrong?"

"It's Charly." She ran a hand through her hair. "She got in trouble in school today, and is on a week's detention."

"What did she do?"

"She didn't do her homework and got mouthy with the teacher when she questioned her about it."

He pursed his lips. "She's going to have to be punished."

"I know, but I don't think we should be too severe." Her eyes pleaded with him. "She's had so much stress in her life lately. I think the school's week of detention is enough."

"She has everything she could want. She should learn gratitude." His jaw twitched. "Now, don't go babying her, Farrel. When someone commits a crime, they need to be punished."

"She didn't commit a crime. You act like she committed murder. Robert. We need to talk to her and find out what's going on with her. She's always been an excellent student and has never been in trouble before."

"That's how it starts. I think Karla Miller is a bad influence on her." He pulled on his chin. "Maybe we shouldn't allow Charly to associate with her anymore."

"Come on, Robert. Karla and Charly have been friends for years. We have no right to choose her friends for her. Besides, it's not Karla's fault that Charly didn't do her homework." Farrel knew the reason Charly hadn't done it was because of what had happened last night. As far as she was concerned, she wasn't going to punish Charly at all...the punishment from school was enough, and that was even more severe than she felt her daughter deserved. She closely watched Robert's eyes, wondering which direction he would go.

"Well, we'll think of something. But right now, I have some news I think will make you very happy." He smiled broadly.

"What?" she asked, unsure of his cheerful mood.

"I set us up with a marriage counselor today," he said.

She returned his smile. "I know this will be a turning point for us. Once we work through all of our problems, I'm sure our marriage will be what we always dreamed it should be."

Robert lifted an eyebrow. "Well, he had a cancellation, so we lucked out. We have an appointment for tomorrow afternoon. We'll be seeing Ben Holbrook. He comes highly recommended."

"Did his receptionist ask what kind of problems we're having, or any questions, Robert?" she asked.

"Yes. I said that we have a communication problem. She said that's common, especially in second marriages."

"Okay." She turned to the stove. "Could you help me with dinner?"

"Sure, what do you need?" He put an arm around her waist.

"Just set the table, honey." She stirred a pot full of vegetables. "I'm getting pretty good with only one arm," she joked.

Robert raised his eyebrows. "Ummm…maybe we'll see how good you are later on."

<<<>>>

"Did you decide what you want to do tonight, Frankie?" Gary asked.

"Let's just stay here. I'd feel better. There's a good movie on tonight."

"How are things?" he asked as he followed her into the living room. "Is everything okay?"

"It's weird. Robert and my mom are going for counseling tomorrow. They're acting like a normal husband and wife."

"Isn't that all you've ever wanted?" he asked. "Maybe Robert realizes he went too far."

She frowned. "Yeah, but Robert's acting so phony. I don't buy it. He's being nice, but I can tell he doesn't really mean it." She threw her hands up in exasperation. "It's so tense, just waiting for the inevitable explosion to occur."

"Maybe you're looking for something that isn't there," he reasoned. "Like I said, could be Robert realizes what he's done and is afraid your mother might go to the police or something."

"You're right. I should relax and enjoy the peace while it lasts." She grabbed his hand. "Let's sit down and check out the movie."

Gary followed her to the sofa and sat next to her. "Where is everybody?"

"Robert and my mother went to Bobby's baseball game, and Charly and Karla Miller are in Charly's room."

"So, we have some privacy, huh?" He grinned as he put an arm around her. "About time."

"Behave yourself, Mr. Blackmon," she teased as she clicked the TV on.

"Do we need all of these lights on, Frankie?" he asked as he nuzzled her shoulder with his chin.

"I don't think so." She playfully jabbed him in his ribs. "If you think you can control yourself."

"I'll try, but you are tempting. Did you know that?"

"Well, I certainly don't feel like I am," she answered as

she clicked off the lights.

"You need to have a positive attitude. You should see yourself like everyone else does, Frankie. I wish I could convince you how special you are to me and how much I love you." His voice was soft.

"I love you, too, Gary," she whispered. She looked into his coal black eyes, then lowered her head and planted a kiss on his neck. "I just wish things were different around here." She sighed. "I never know from one day to the next what's going to happen to my mom."

"I thought you were going to relax," Gary reminded her.

"You're right."

He held her tighter. "Did you know that I liked you before you even knew I existed?"

"You *did*?" Her eyes widened.

"Yes, I did."

"Then why didn't you ever say anything to me?" she asked as she smiled up at him.

"You were hung up on Jake Richards. I figured I wouldn't stand a chance compared to a guy like him."

"Give me a break. That was just a childish short-lived infatuation. Every girl in school was crazy about him. But after I got to know him, it didn't take long to see what a conceited jerk he really was." She touched Gary's cheek. "And just for the record, I had a crush on *you* for a long time."

He smiled. "Well, I'm just glad you said you'd go out with me when I finally got up the nerve to ask you out."

She grinned. "How come you make me feel so good about myself?"

"Because I love you." He bent his head and softly kissed her.

Frankie's heartbeat quickened, and feelings began to stir

in her. She wrapped her arms tighter around his neck and pressed her body against his. She was oblivious to anything or anyone but Gary and wasn't even aware when they'd moved from an upright position to a horizontal position. Frankie always managed to stop before things got out of control, and she wouldn't let things get out of control tonight either.

"What the hell is going on?" Robert's voice thundered as he flicked on the lamp and walked to the sofa. His face was red with anger as he grabbed Gary's shoulder.

CHAPTER FOUR

Gary jumped to an upright position. "Hi, Mr. Drake." His eyes shifted nervously. "I guess we must have dozed off watching TV."

Frankie sat up and looked Robert squarely in the eye. "We didn't do anything." Her voice was defensive.

Robert eyed her suspiciously. "I think you'd better leave, Gary," he ordered. "Now!"

"Hey, what's going on?" Charly asked as she entered the room with Karla on her heels.

"Gary and Frankie were going at it on the couch," Bobby sneered. "Dad caught 'em."

"We were not!" Frankie said indignantly.

"Like they're going to do something with Karla and me in the next room. No one is that stupid. You're just jealous, Bobby, because you couldn't find anyone to go out with you if you paid her," Charly said in defense of her sister.

Karla giggled as she nudged Charly. "No one's that desperate."

Farrel saw Robert's jaw tighten, and she knew by the narrowing of his eyes that he was ready to explode. She had to take control of the situation. "Charly, you're grounded — or did you forget?"

Charly looked into her mother's eyes and picked up the

clue. She turned to Karla. "You'd better go. I'll see you in school."

Karla gave Robert a hard look and then turned to Farrel. "Hope your arm heals soon, Mrs. Drake," she said as she grabbed her jacket.

"I'd better be going, too," Gary said, obviously hoping to escape Robert's wrath.

"Just a minute." Robert laid a heavy hand on Gary's shoulder. "I don't *ever* want to see you and Frankie in that type of situation again. Do I make myself clear?"

"We weren't doing anything wrong." Gary shifted awkwardly from foot to foot.

"I've heard that one before. I'll be watching you. You can count on it!" Robert's voice was cold.

Frankie grabbed Gary's arm and led him to the door. "I'm sorry," she whispered.

"He'd better not lay a finger on you," Gary warned. "God help him if he does." He kissed her cheek. "See you tomorrow."

Robert turned on his heel and faced Farrel. "So, you bailed them out again." His eyes slanted as they bore into hers.

"I don't understand what you mean. I didn't do anything, Robert." She tried to keep her voice light.

"That's just it. My son, as usual, has to put up not only with insults from your daughters but their friends as well."

"You know how kids are, Robert." She touched his arm. "Besides, he picks on them as much as they do him. They're kids."

Robert rolled his eyes. "Sure. Stick up for them as usual." He shrugged off her hand and walked over to his son. "That was a great game, Bobby." He slapped him on the back. "You'll always find others who are jealous of you." He turned his head and stared at Farrel but directed his next statement to his son. "The girls can't stand it because they know how much better you are than them, son. You'll go far in life, but I doubt they'll succeed at anything."

"Someday they'll be sorry, Dad. I'll be the one laughing at them."

"That's for sure. God will punish them for every rotten thing they've ever said or done to you."

Farrel couldn't believe her ears. "Robert, don't forget all of the things Bobby has done to them. Remember, if you point a finger, you'll have three pointing back at you," she stated quietly.

Robert laughed. "Remember your words, Farrel, the next time you accuse me of things I haven't done."

Farrel shook her head in disgust before turning her attention to Bobby. "I'm sure the girls were only teasing you the same way you tease them," she added softly. "They meant no harm."

"Sure. Like Dad says, you always stick up for the girls. You don't care what happens to me." He glared at her with the same cold, dark eyes of his father. "You just try to make everybody think that Dad is a bad guy, but you never tell them what you do to him!"

"It's not true. I do care what happens to you, Bobby." Her eyes softened as she looked at him. She wondered what he was really thinking. Was he remembering how she had always treated him with kindness even when he didn't deserve it? He was in turmoil—Farrel sensed it. She could only keep trying to reach the part of him that Robert hadn't hardened. She'd been trying to dig the good out of him and had made some progress, but she feared Bobby's emotional damage went much deeper, and she would never fully succeed.

Bobby shrugged his shoulders. "As if I would ever believe a word you say." His voice was sarcastic. "Dad and I got along great before he got mixed up with you!" His eyes darkened.

Farrel sighed. "I'd never lie to you, Bobby. And deep down I think you know that."

Robert grunted. "Just give it up, Farrel. Your actions have proved where your true loyalties lie. My son and I will never mean anything to you. Whenever something goes wrong, you either put all the blame on him or me. Not once have you *ever* properly disciplined your daughters."

"That's not true, Robert. But I can see this conversation is going nowhere, so let's end it."

"Why don't you take a shower, son? I've got to give Charly her punishment for getting into trouble at school today."

"She's been punished enough, Robert."

"Not nearly," he replied.

He looked at Farrel, challenging her with his eyes to say something, but she kept silent. She followed him down the hall to Frankie and Charly's room. She wouldn't allow him to lay a hand on her daughter. If he did, that would be the last straw.

Robert opened the door.

"Hey, don't you believe in knocking?" Charly demanded. She was sprawled across her bed, staring at a fashion magazine.

"I pay the rent, young lady, and whenever I want to enter this room, I will, without permission from you or anyone else!" Robert boomed.

Charly looked at him, surprised, and then turned her attention to her mother. "Mom, I deserve some privacy. What if I was changing my clothes?"

Farrel grabbed Robert's arm. "Honey, she's right. We shouldn't invade the kids' privacy. We wouldn't want them barging into our room any time they felt like it," she reasoned.

Robert's eyes flashed as he pushed his wife's hand from his arm. "There you go again, Farrel, always defending them and making me out to be some kind of a monster!" He walked over to Charly. "I will not tolerate any more of your backtalk! After the stunt you pulled in school today you are grounded for a month—no TV, stereo, nothing! Do I make myself clear?"

Charly pursed her lips. "Give me a break! All I did was forget a stupid assignment! I didn't commit murder!"

"Any more of your mouth, and I'll double it!"

"Robert," Farrel said, "don't you think you're going overboard with the punishment?"

"Stay out of it, Farrel! I'm the head of this house, and it's about time you got that through your thick skull!" He angrily pointed a finger at her.

His finger was almost touching her face. "Please don't point your finger at me, Robert. I can't stand that."

"Don't you ever tell me what I can or cannot do in my own home!" He pushed her roughly away from him, causing her cast-laden arm to thud against the wall.

Farrel clenched her teeth together to suppress her pain.

"Look what you did to Mom!" Charly yelled. "Are you all right, Mom?"

Farrel clenched her teeth. "I'll be fine, honey."

"It was an accident. I would never intentionally hurt your mother! God will punish you for your lies!"

"You're the liar!" Charly shouted back. "If God's going to punish anyone, it's going to be you for the way you treat us."

"I should break your neck!" Robert's nostrils flared as he moved toward the bed.

"Robert!" Farrel shouted. "Don't you dare lay one finger on her!"

Robert abruptly turned on his heel and glared at his wife.

Farrel didn't flinch as he glowered at her. Her eyes met his head on. Her anger was mounting, and if she didn't find a way to push it back down like she always did, it would come pouring out, and she doubted she had the energy to control it after all the years of abuse. And why should she control it? As she continued to stare into his eyes, she wondered if he felt the heat of her anger. She'd never challenged him like this before, and it felt good even though she might pay for it later.

"Run to Mommy, baby," Robert taunted. "You aren't worth the effort. Do what you want. I have tried to be a good father to you, but everything I do for you, you just throw back in my face." He threw his hands up. "I'm done."

"Good," Charly retorted.

"Remember your punishment. Also, you'd better tell Karla Miller that she isn't welcome in my home anymore after her rudeness to my son."

"I thought you were done," Charly reminded him.

Robert's lips tightened. "You'd better watch your step."

Charly rolled her eyes. "Whatever."

<<<>>>

Robert stared at the ceiling. He took a deep breath and held it for a few seconds before exhaling. Farrel lay silently next to him. He was tense, and she knew a battle was raging within him to keep his temper in check. She was so tired—not physically, but mentally. She couldn't take much more and realized that at any moment she would snap, and that would be the end. Her nerves were a twisted, mangled mass of frustrations, but she still clung to one hope. The hope that the marriage counselor would shed some light on how she could help her husband to help himself and how they could hopefully work together to become a normal family. Still, a major part of her recognized that she shouldn't get her hopes too high. Every time she did, Robert pulled the rug out from under her. This time she wouldn't allow it.

<<<>>>

Charly stared at the crumpled pass she held in her hand for a few seconds and then shoved it in her pocket, wondering why Mrs. Browning wanted to see her. As the minutes quietly ticked by, she squirmed on the bench outside of the guidance counselor's office, nervously picking at a fingernail.

The office door suddenly opened, and an attractive young woman peered out. "Charly Stuart?" Mrs. Browning asked.

Charly nodded.

"Come in, please." She held the door.

Charly nervously waited as the woman closed the door, then motioned her to a chair.

"You're probably wondering why I asked to see you this morning," Mrs. Browning said as she observed Charly's uneasiness.

"Is it because of what happened in math class yesterday? I accepted my punishment, and my parents punished me, too."

"No, it's not about that," the woman answered quickly, "but I was surprised. It was out of character for you." She frowned. "I've never known you to get in any trouble in school."

"It won't happen again." She averted her gaze from Mrs. Browning's friendly eyes. She drew a long breath as she waited for Mrs. Browning to explain why she'd called her to the office. The woman took her sweet time replying. Charly finally glanced timidly at her as she shifted in her seat.

"I summoned you here for a different reason, Charly," she finally said. "One of your friends is very concerned about you. Is there anything you'd like to talk about?"

Charly bit her bottom lip as she peered at Mrs. Browning. "No, everything's fine." She glanced around the perfectly organized office. Everything had a place, and everything was in it. The woman obviously was a neat freak. "So who asked you to talk to me?"

Mrs. Browning walked to her comfortable looking but dainty chair and stood with her hands on the back of it. "It doesn't really matter who asked me. This person is very concerned about your welfare."

"It had to be Karla Miller. What did she say?"

Mrs. Browning's tone grew serious. "I'm not divulging any names, Charly. As I said, it doesn't matter who asked me. Your friend is very worried about you and is afraid that coming to me could cause you further trouble, but had no other choice. Would you like to address this person's concerns?"

"There's nothing to address," Charly quickly said. "I know it's Karla who came to you. She's my closest friend, but I wish she hadn't talked to you." She swallowed hard. "I don't know why she'd be concerned since there's nothing unusual going on in my life."

Mrs. Browning sat and glanced briefly at the files on her desk before moving her eyes back to Charly. "Would you like to talk about anything in particular, Charly?"

She shrugged. "No."

"How are things at home?"

She cleared her throat and pasted a phony smile on her face. "Good. Probably the same as everybody else's." She stared at the woman. "What did Karla tell you?"

Mrs. Browning was quiet for a long minute. "I understand your parents are having some difficulties."

"Not my mom." She dropped her eyes. "I don't want to talk about my family."

"Your stepfather, then?" the woman persisted.

Charly cleared her throat again. "I need to get to class."

"Charly, something is bothering you. We're here to help you."

"Sometimes helping only makes things worse, Mrs. Browning," Her eyes misted.

"I don't know what you mean."

Charly met her eyes. "I think you do. The consequences of anything I say could end up being worse for me."

"Is someone threatening you, Charly?" Mrs. Browning asked quietly.

Charly drew a shaky breath, stood, and walked over to the window. She stared out at the parking lot for a few seconds and then turned back and faced Mrs. Browning. "My stepfather is always beating on my mother." Her voice quivered. "A couple of nights ago he broke her arm." Tears filled her eyes.

Mrs. Browning quickly rose and walked over to Charly. She put a friendly arm around her shoulder. "I think I'll have your sister join us."

Charly nodded.

<<<>>>

Farrel gazed at her reflection in the full-length mirror. She looked pale, so she added more blush to her hollow cheeks. She noticed how thin she was becoming. Her eyes no longer held their shiny gleam; now, they looked tired and vacant. The counseling had to work. She needed to hold on to something. She selected a skirt that was a favorite of Robert's and a plain cotton blouse. Farrel dabbed some perfume behind her ears, then carefully applied her lipstick. She frowned at her appearance. If it weren't for her cast, she would look almost presentable, she thought. Now all she had to do was wait for

Robert to pick her up.

<<<>>>

"What's wrong?" Frankie asked nervously as she walked into Mrs. Browning's office.

"I had you summoned, Frankie, because I'd like to talk to you and your sister," the counselor said.

Frankie looked questioningly at the woman. "Is everything all right, Charly?" she asked as she walked over to the window where Charly was still standing.

"I told her about Robert," Charly said in a low voice.

Frankie stiffened. What had Charly said? She couldn't question her sister in front of Mrs. Browning. Her heart pounded in her chest. They wouldn't be safe from Robert if he found out. Charly should have kept her mouth shut until their mother got them safely away from him. It hadn't seemed to Frankie that her mother was making much of an effort in that department, though. She'd thought after the broken arm incident her mother would have immediately left him. But then again, it was difficult to leave when you had no money or nowhere to go. She had to cut her mother some slack.

"Everything will be fine," Mrs. Browning assured Frankie, "Charly told me that your stepfather broke your mother's arm. I wanted to talk to you about that."

Frankie nodded. She couldn't make up an excuse, and suddenly she didn't want to anymore. Robert should pay for the hell he was putting them through.

"Has he abused you girls in any way?"

Frankie and Charly looked hesitantly at each other. "He used to smack us around, but now he only makes threats," Frankie finally said. "My mother put a stop to it."

"How about your mother?"

"My mother has never abused us," Charly said

emphatically.

"No, she's very good to us. In fact, she takes a lot to protect us," Frankie explained.

Mrs. Browning frowned. "Has he ever hurt your mother in front of you girls?"

"Yes," Frankie whispered. "Verbally and physically."

"Your mother doesn't have to put up with it. There is help available."

"They're going to a counselor today," Charly said. "I doubt it'll do much good, though."

"Has your mother ever pressed charges?"

"No, but we stayed in a shelter for a few weeks," Frankie explained. "When we went back home, things were okay for a while, but then Robert, my stepfather, started in again."

Mrs. Browning's voice was sympathetic. "Please keep me informed if anything changes at home. And please notify me immediately if your stepfather touches either of you girls." She smiled sympathetically at them. "I only want to help you two."

"Please don't tell anyone what we told you, Mrs. Browning," Frankie pleaded. "If you report it, we'll have to deny it." Her eyes brimmed. "And we don't want to lie because we really like you. But what choice will we have?"

<<<>>>

Farrel sat on a light blue plush chair next to an identical chair where Robert was seated. Ben Holbrook sat on a small dark blue couch across from them. A small table separated them. The walls were painted a pale blue with very few wall decorations. The office was small but decorated to give a homey feel to it. Farrel supposed it was to make clients feel more relaxed.

"So, tell me why you two are here," Ben Holbrook said

as he picked up a pen and a legal pad and waited for one of them to speak.

Robert looked at Farrel. "I'll start if I may."

"Go ahead," the doctor said.

"My wife is jealous of any relationship I have with my family," he said.

Farrel's eyes widened in surprise. "That's not true, Robert. You know that."

"It *is* true, Farrel." He looked at Holbrook. "She can't tolerate me caring about anyone but her. I love and respect my mother, and she can't stand it."

"You're lying, Robert. Your family has accused me of things I've never done." She looked at Ben Holbrook. "I have tried to be accepted by his family, but they shut me out. They refuse to have anything to do with me. As far as Robert's mother is concerned, I am *not* jealous of her. He should love and respect his mother. But that doesn't mean he has to agree with the lies his mother has made up about me."

Ben Holbrook stared hard at her for a few seconds. "Farrel, isn't it true that you took drugs and had an affair with one of Robert's relatives before you met Robert?" His voice was unsympathetic.

Farrel felt like someone had plunged a knife through her heart. "No, it isn't!" Tears glistened in her eyes. "Robert's mother started that rumor when Robert and I first met. I don't know what her problem is where I'm concerned. I've tried to get along with her. I swore to Robert over and over none of the things she told him were true, but he refuses to believe me. That hurts." She looked at her husband, who had a smug expression on his face. "I refuse to be accused of things I didn't do."

Ben Holbrook shifted his heavy body on the couch as he

watched her. He was tall with a commanding personality, in his mid-forties, with graying hair on his head and around his temples. "Calm down, Farrel, no one is accusing you of anything. I just want you to understand why Robert feels betrayed by you. If you had been open with him about your past when you two first met, I'm sure that his mother wouldn't have dug up information about you."

Farrel couldn't believe what she was hearing. She'd been set up! Robert had set her up! "But it isn't true!" she repeated. "You told me I wasn't being accused of anything, but you've already made it clear that you're on Robert's side. It doesn't matter what I say. My girls and I had to live in a shelter because Robert's family convinced him to throw us out! What kind of man does that to his wife?"

Robert shook his head as he looked at the older man. "I told you she has mental problems. She even tried to have me committed to an institution once, but my family intervened."

"That never happened. How can you sit there and lie, Robert?" Tears filled her eyes. "What about my arm? What about the bruises on my body?" she screamed.

"Calm down, Farrel," Ben Holbrook ordered. "I'm here to help you, but if you continue to shout, it will accomplish nothing." His voice was stern.

"Have you spoken to Robert prior to today?" Farrel demanded.

"That's not important," the doctor answered.

"Yes, it is. You didn't answer me about my broken arm and bruises."

"I told him about your clumsiness, Farrel," Robert said calmly. "How can you sit there and accuse me of things I never did?"

"My daughters have witnessed your abuse."

"They'll say anything you want them to," Robert replied.

"Are you harboring a suppressed resentment against your husband because of something that has happened in your past, Farrel, and are now taking it out on him?"

"I don't believe this," Farrel said as she stood up. "I won't listen to any more of these lies and accusations!" She walked to the door. "This is a waste of time. You've already talked to Robert, and made up your mind about me before I even came here."

"Farrel, get back here!" the doctor ordered. "This outburst of yours isn't helping."

She turned and stared at Ben Holbrook, then said, "No, this is all a ridiculous pack of lies, and I won't listen to any more."

<<<>>>

Farrel dabbed at her eyes with a tissue. "How could you do that to me, Robert?" Her voice shook. "How could you set me up?" Her emotional pain was almost unbearable. "You lied to me and about me."

"Oh, get a grip, Farrel. You get so emotional. Can't you see how you made a fool of yourself in front of Ben Holbrook?" He threw his hands up in exasperation. "The guy thinks you're a mental case!"

"I won't listen to any more lies from you, Robert!" Her insides quivered, and she was overcome with a feeling of emptiness and loneliness, which seemed to engulf her more with every word Robert spoke.

"You *will* listen, Farrel." He grabbed her shoulders and shook her so hard she thought her neck would snap.

"Stop it!" Farrel placed the palm of her good hand on his chest and pushed at him with all the strength she could muster. "I won't let you hurt me again." Her eyes flashed angrily. "Someday, you'll have to face the consequences of what you have done, Robert. But I will not allow you to ever hurt my daughters or me again. I must have been crazy to have allowed this for all these years." She paused to catch her breath. "But I'll tell you something," she said, her voice rising with each word. "You are the cruelest man I have ever met! You don't have blood running through those veins of yours — you have ice water!" Her heart was thumping furiously when she finished. She looked at him and couldn't believe his reaction. He was sneering at her.

Robert shook his head. "I feel sorry for you, Farrel. You never could take criticism. Whenever something doesn't go your way, you go off the deep end." He chuckled. "No one would ever believe the stories you make up about me. I have a good reputation, and you are only going to destroy your life by making up these crazy stories."

Farrel didn't know whether to laugh or to cry, but there was no way she could back down now. If she did, Robert would abuse and torment her for the rest of her life. And most importantly, how could she ever live with herself if she didn't stand firm? She would lose everything if she let him win, and she would end up destroyed. She wouldn't let Robert keep her in this prison. She had to break free. It was time.

"I don't want you to bring this topic up ever again, Farrel. Do I make myself clear? I will never go to counseling with you again after you embarrassed me!"

"Robert, please!" She felt a lump catch in her throat. "Why can't you for once in your life just admit what you've done? I'm trying to help you!"

Robert rolled his eyes. "Farrel, I have told you over and over that your imagination is going to get you into trouble. You can't falsely accuse someone of violent behavior. You'll find yourself in serious trouble someday," he warned.

"Robert, maybe you can convince everyone else you are innocent, but just remember, I know the truth. As God is my witness, Robert, I will not tolerate any more of your lies and abuse. You have convinced your family and the church that I am to blame for all of our problems." Her voice trembled. "How could you do that? How could you tell such horrible, vicious lies about me? Why, Robert? I have tried so hard to make this marriage work, but I just can't take any more." She stared into his cold, jeering eyes. "You need help, Robert. Do yourself and Bobby a favor and get help for the both of you."

He started to laugh. "Listen to yourself. You twist everything. If it isn't Farrel's way, it's no one's way. You are so sick!" He grabbed her arm. "Do you remember the time you called my family over and tried to convince them that I was abusing you and your daughters?" His voice was loud.

"I called them because you were acting like a maniac."

"Right! You and your girls attacked *me*! I was trying to defend myself!" he shouted.

Farrel pulled her arm free. "No, you are lying! You were like a crazy man that night. How can you lie about it?" She looked incredulously at him. "You think you can do whatever you want to me and the girls. You always get bailed out, don't you?" Farrel didn't wait for an answer, but continued as all the suppressed anger she had felt for so long came pouring out. "Your family has covered for you from the first day I met you! They saw you beat me and then acted as though it was my fault because you were under stress! I must have provoked you, they said. It's always the same thing, Robert. You do the same thing where Bobby and the girls are concerned. Do you recall the time you humiliated Charly by making her sit at the kitchen table for two hours because she wouldn't finish her dinner?" Her eyes filled with tears at the recollection. "She kept telling you she wasn't feeling well, but you refused to listen. You were like a madman ranting and raving. Then to make matters worse, Bobby had a friend over who happened to be a classmate of Charly's. Instead of asking him to leave, you continued to berate Charly in front of everybody!"

Farrel lowered her voice. "I watched you, Robert. I watched your eyes. They were filled with something evil. Then when I comforted my own child, you stormed into the living room and pouted like a child, insisting that I was interfering with your duty as head of the household. You remember, Robert, I know you do!" She glared at him. "You tried to twist it and make me feel guilty like you were innocent. It's always your feelings that come first. As long as you're happy, it doesn't matter how anyone else feels. Like the incident with Charly. The next night Bobby wasted most of his dinner, and you never said a word to him. When I questioned you about it, you told me to leave him alone and to get off his back." Her eyes were cold as she continued to stare at him. "I can't take anymore, Robert. Either you get some help or —"

"Or what?" Robert thundered. "I've listened to you for the past ten minutes, and as usual, you don't appreciate a thing I've done for you." He pointed a finger at her. "And don't you ever threaten me! My whole family knows what I've put up with all these years with you! You need help, not me!"

Farrel looked disgustedly at him. "I might as well save my breath. You'll never admit what you do." She walked towards the kitchen. "I've got to start dinner."

Chapter Five

"So how'd your parents' counseling go?" Gary asked as he bit into his sandwich.

Frankie stared at the tray of uneaten food in front of her. "Not well. All they did was fight all night."

"You look exhausted. Didn't get much sleep, huh?"

Frankie sighed. "Not much. It wasn't really because of their fighting, though. I was just afraid he'd hurt my mom again." She moved the vegetables on her plate around with her spoon. "I don't know what to do, Gary. I'm so sick of it."

"Have you asked your mom to leave him?"

"Yeah, but she doesn't have any money. Only our child support. There's no way we could make it on that." Tears sparkled in her eyes. "There's got to be a way, Gary."

"Maybe she could get a job."

"We still need to have a place to live. There's no way she can come up with a security deposit and first and last month's rent."

Gary was thoughtful for a few minutes as he chewed on his sandwich. "What if Robert moved out and your mother got to stay in the apartment?"

"I never thought of that," Frankie replied, brightening. "Then she could get a job."

"Did Robert do anything to you last night?"

"No, he was still ranting about Charly getting into trouble at school the other day." She sighed.

"He didn't hit her, did he?" he asked angrily. "I know I tease Charly a lot, but I really do care about her."

"No. He was yelling at my mom about her." Frankie put a hand over his. "I think he would have hit her the other night if my mom hadn't stopped him. As it is, he grounded her for a ridiculous length of time and took away TV, phone, and stereo privileges. And she can't see Karla anymore."

"What a jerk." He shook his head. "I just hope your mother can think of something to get you guys away from him."

"Me, too, Gary. Me, too."

<<<>>>

"What happened after I left the other night?" Karla asked as she flipped open her math book.

"Robert took away my TV, stereo, phone—everything."

"That's stupid. For how long?"

"A month." She turned around and noticed that Miss Wymer hadn't entered the room yet. She returned her attention to Karla. "There's one more thing," she said quietly.

"What?"

Charly frowned. "I'm not supposed to see you anymore. Robert thinks you're a bad influence."

Karla's forehead wrinkled. "So, the evil one doesn't like me, huh?"

Charly saw through her friend's sarcasm and right to the hurt she knew Karla must be feeling. Karla always had a knack for hiding her true feelings behind a mask of sarcasm. Only those who knew her well knew how insecure she really was. "We can still get together after school and stuff," she said.

"I thought you were grounded."

"Yeah, but I'll blow that off. Besides, I think my mom is

planning something."

"What do you mean?"

Charly smiled. "I think she's getting ready to leave Robert. They didn't have any luck with their counseling. They fought half the night over it."

"He didn't hit your mom again, did he?"

"No."

"I like your mom, Charly, and I really hope that you guys dump the evil one and the little twerp."

Charly laughed. "Bobby is such a wimp. The way he cries to Daddy all the time. But sometimes I feel sorry for him having Robert for a father."

Karla made a face. "I guess so, but it still doesn't excuse the way he acts."

Out of the corner of her eye, Charly spotted Miss Wymer entering the room. "I'll talk to you later," she whispered.

<<<>>>

Farrel rested on her knees as she pulled a few weeds from her garden with her good arm.

"Hi, Farrel."

She glanced up into the warm, friendly eyes of Betty Levitt. "Hi, Betty," she answered, returning the smile.

"How's the arm doing?"

Farrel stood up. "Not too bad, but it sure is inconvenient. It's frustrating trying to get the simplest things done."

"Do you need any help?" Betty offered.

"Oh, no, thank you," Farrel quickly replied. "The kids and Robert are doing a great job. In fact, I'm kind of enjoying being pampered." She laughed.

"Can I talk to you for a few minutes?" Betty asked.

"Of course."

"It's personal."

Farrel wondered what Betty wanted to discuss with her. She became uneasy as Betty's penetrating eyes looked at her. *She knows the truth*, she thought. *She must have heard Robert and me arguing again.* "I...uh...sure, I guess," she finally muttered.

Betty put a friendly hand on Farrel's shoulder. "Come to my apartment for a cold glass of lemonade."

Farrel nervously looked around herself as though she expected to see Robert's cold, threatening eyes warning her not to get too friendly. She slowly followed the woman past the rows of gardens and into the building. Before she knew it, she found herself seated on the sofa in Betty Levitt's living room with a tall, cold glass of lemonade clutched tightly in her hand.

"I'm pleased that you've finally agreed to visit me." Betty sat in a chair facing Farrel. She set her glass of lemonade on a coaster on top of the coffee table. "I want to be your friend, Farrel, but you don't seem to want to get close to anyone. I've watched you ever since you've moved in here, and you spend all your time alone." Her voice was soft.

Farrel rapidly blinked her eyes, fighting the tears that threatened to fall. She knew if she didn't collect herself immediately, she would end up pouring her heart out to Betty Levitt. And if she did, Robert might find out, and Farrel didn't know how she would deal with him. But then, her mind tried to reason, why should she care? She'd already warned Robert that she would never allow him to hurt her ever again. After all the lies he told about her to everyone, she had the right to let one person know the hell she was living. And she so desperately needed a friend. Betty was more than a friend; she was a mother image. Farrel needed a mother since her own mother had passed away a couple of years earlier.

Farrel recalled the pain and humiliation Robert had

caused her at her mother's funeral. He had ignored her and the girls and had refused to talk to any of her relatives. If one didn't know better, they might think he was jealous of the attention she was bestowing on her deceased mother. No one from his family offered their condolences. Farrel had felt so alone. When she had needed Robert the most to lean on, he had pulled away. His rudeness toward the mourners embarrassed her, and she tried to make excuses for him, but his lack of friendliness toward her family only led them to further their negative opinion of him. Especially since several months before her mother's death her grandmother had passed away, and Robert had refused to attend the funeral with her. He said he had to pick up a specially designed gift for Bobby, and there was no other time he could schedule to get it.

As Farrel thought about all the painful memories with Robert, her eyes flooded, and soon hot heavy tears zigzagged down her cheeks. Her grief consumed her, and she temporarily forgot that she was sitting in Betty Levitt's living room. She cried so hard her chest heaved as though she were gasping for air. She couldn't stop the horrible memories flooding through her mind one at a time; the pain suffocated her.

Betty Levitt was quickly at her side with a box of tissues. She put both arms around Farrel and held her close, being careful of Farrel's broken arm. "It'll be all right," she whispered as she stroked Farrel's hair. She sat for twenty minutes comforting Farrel, until Farrel's tears finally subsided.

"I'm sorry," Farrel sniffed. "I'm just exhausted."

"Don't apologize, dear," Betty replied in a soft voice. "Whatever is inside of you must be terribly painful. I'm not prying, Farrel, but I just want you to know if you ever need a friend to talk to, I'm a good listener."

Farrel took a tissue and dabbed at her eyes. "I don't usually break down like this." She took a long, shuddering breath. "I've just been under so much stress lately."

"Farrel, I won't lie to you," she began slowly. "The walls in this building are very thin. I, as well as several others, have heard what goes on in your apartment," she said frankly.

Farrel's face flushed. "I...I don't know what to say." She knew she had to say something. Betty had just admitted that their fights were known throughout the building. If she kept her silence, then Betty might think she was the cause of Robert's and her problems. "Betty, things aren't always as they seem."

<<<>>>

Betty could see the pain in Farrel's eyes. She silently prayed that Farrel would trust her. For two long years, she had watched the pretty young woman struggle with loneliness. She saw it in Farrel's eyes every time they happened to pass one another. And she saw it in the shy smile Farrel would offer. She'd told her husband, Bill, so many times that if someone didn't intervene, something horrible would happen in the Drake apartment. The arguments were growing more frequent and more intense. She was surprised no one had ever called the police, but like Bill said, why bring more trouble on the Drakes? Betty patted Farrel's arm. "You don't have to say anything. Just know that I am always here if you need me."

Farrel sighed tiredly. "I can't take it anymore," she blurted out. "My husband and I are having problems. We went to a marriage counselor, and I was hoping it would work, but I was set up." Her words came out in a rush, and she knew she probably made no sense.

"Farrel, every marriage has its own problems. It takes a lot of time and effort to make a marriage work, especially in these times," she said.

"No, this is different. I can't do anything to please Robert. He finds fault with everything." Her eyes brimmed with tears again.

"Does he forbid you to have friends?" Betty asked.

Her eyes narrowed. "He doesn't like me to get close to anyone. He says that people will just cause problems between us."

"But, Farrel, everybody needs someone to lean on. You can't isolate yourself," Betty reasoned.

"That's the point," Farrel explained. "Every time I try to get close to anyone, Robert ruins the friendship." A tear slid down her cheek. "I'm so lonely, Betty. And I'm scared."

Betty patted Farrel's arm. "I'll be your friend, Farrel. I'll help you get through it."

"But Robert will be furious if he finds out I'm talking to you."

Betty sensed Farrel's fear and loneliness. "We won't let him find out," she said. "It'll be our secret."

"I shouldn't have to sneak around to have a friend. No one else has to. For years I've watched friends doing things together, and I've felt so left out." Tears streamed down her cheeks. "When we moved here, I thought that finally, he would let me have a friend since this building houses so many apartments. But he warned me not to get involved. You don't know how hard it is for me day after day to come outside and work on my garden and watch everyone pull up chairs and visit. And when you invited me in for coffee, I wanted to accept, but I was too afraid of what Robert would do." She choked back sobs.

Betty's heart ached for Farrel. She looked into Farrel's red, swollen eyes, then at the cast on her arm and the faint bruises on her cheek and other arm. "Farrel, can I ask you a very personal question? You don't have to answer me if you don't want to."

"What is it?" Farrel whispered.

"Your bruises...did Robert cause them? Remember the first time we talked, and you told me you bumped into the kitchen cupboard? And then, when you broke your arm, you said that you slipped on the kitchen floor."

Farrel lowered her eyes.

"Did your husband do that to you?"

Farrel's eyes widened. "Please don't tell anyone. You don't know Robert's temper."

"I won't say anything," Betty quickly reassured her. "I only want to help you." She patted her arm. "What about your family, Farrel? Have you told them anything? Can't they offer you some emotional support?"

She took a deep breath. "My mother passed away some time ago. I have several brothers and sisters, but we've drifted apart. They have their own lives and problems. And Robert made it clear after our marriage that they were not welcome in our home." She frowned. "Robert is very possessive. He can do whatever he wants when he wants, but if I want to do something, he accuses me of not caring for him. Over a period of time, I gave up my friends and everything I liked to do. When my mother was still alive, he became jealous that I was spending too much time with her. But the ironic thing is that he spends as much time with his family as he wants to."

"That's not a normal relationship, Farrel," Betty said, as her mind tried to comprehend the hell Farrel must be enduring each day with no relief in sight. She knew this woman needed help badly if she were to survive much longer. "How does his family treat you?" Betty asked.

"Not well. His mother is jealous of me." She watched Betty's eyebrows raise. "I know it sounds strange," she explained, "but it's the truth. It's almost as though she wants him just for herself. She caused problems for us, but Robert will not admit it. He will defend his mother with his life." She sighed. "I tried so hard to form a relationship with her, but she is so cold to me and my daughters. She showers Bobby with gifts in front of the girls and lets them know in subtle ways that she will never accept them as her step-grandchildren. It makes my blood run cold.

"She will not allow the girls to call her grandmother, but my own mother always referred to Bobby as her grandson and never slighted him. Mrs. Drake started some vicious rumors about me, and Robert, of course, believed her. I swore to him none of it was true, but he refused to believe that his mother would lie, even though she couldn't prove her allegations against me. It was about that time he started physically abusing me. He told our pastor and our church family his mother's lies, and they started turning away from me, too. He got his way. He always does. He made me totally dependent on him."

Betty shook her head in wonder. "You said earlier that you and your husband went to a marriage counselor. How did that go?"

"It didn't. It was a waste of time. Robert lied to me again. He set me up, and the counselor accused me of things I never did." She wrung her hands. "Oh, Betty, this must sound crazy to you. You must be thinking that I'm some sort of nut."

"On the contrary," Betty Levitt answered. "There are more women than you think, Farrel, in your situation. Like you, they, too, are victimized. Some of them stay in marriages that are abusive for their entire lives...a virtual prisoner in their own homes."

"I probably shouldn't have told you as much as I did," she said nervously.

"I'm glad you did, Farrel. It's not healthy to keep it all bottled up inside." She patted Farrel's hand. "You still haven't answered my question...did Robert cause your injuries?"

"Yes." She began to cry again.

<<<>>>

Farrel hurried into the apartment and over to the ringing telephone. "Hello," she breathlessly said.

"Good afternoon, Mrs. Drake. I'm Mrs. Browning. I'm a guidance counselor at the high school. I've had a talk with your daughters, Frankie and Charly, and I would like to speak to you." Her voice was friendly.

"They aren't in any trouble, are they?" she asked nervously.

"No.... No, we had a nice visit, and they mentioned a couple of things I'd like to discuss with you. Would it be possible for you to come down to the school this afternoon?"

Farrel bit her bottom lip. "Of course. I'll be there as soon as I can."

<<<>>>

Farrel stared at Mrs. Browning, not knowing what to say.

Maggie Browning offered her a friendly smile. "I'm on your side, Mrs. Drake. Whatever we discuss here is strictly confidential."

Farrel frowned. "I'm not sure I know how to respond." She nervously twisted the strap of her purse.

"Your daughters told me there have been some difficulties at home with their stepfather." She glanced at Farrel's cast.

Farrel felt the heat of embarrassment burning against her cheeks. "Yes, my husband and I are having some problems, but I never thought my daughters would publicly air them."

"Oh, no, I requested that your daughters see me after one of their friends mentioned there might be some serious problems in your home." Her voice was kind. "They were very reluctant to talk at first."

"Who was the friend?" Farrel asked in a shaky voice as she tried to control the fear threatening to engulf her.

"It's confidential, Mrs. Drake." She sighed. "I want to ease your worries. My job is to help in any way I can with any problems you and your daughters may be having, and to help you find resources to obtain aid if needed."

"I thought you were a guidance counselor."

"I am, and my position entitles me to counsel any student or family who asks for my help."

"Did my daughters ask you to contact me?"

"No, but they told me what's been going on."

Farrel slowly shook her head. "I don't blame them for needing to get it off their chests. I suppose I should be grateful that they have such a caring friend." She paused. "My husband and I attended a counseling session, but it didn't go well," she admitted.

"Do you think your husband would be willing to talk to me?"

She shook her head. "The way things went with our session, I don't think he would do it."

"Is there anything I can do for you, Mrs. Drake? I want to help in any way that I can," she repeated.

"How are my girls? I know the things they've been through, but sometimes they might tell someone else their deepest feelings. I do worry about their emotional wellbeing."

"As I said, they were both reluctant to say anything at first, but they definitely are very protective of you. I sensed that they are fearful for your safety."

Farrel took a deep breath. "They have seen things and been through things that no children should ever be exposed to. But I've tried to do what is best for them and raise them with good basic morals."

"Your daughters are intelligent and very well mannered, Mrs. Drake. You've done a wonderful job in rearing them."

"Then what's the problem?" Farrel asked as she stared into the woman's warm, friendly eyes.

"I'm concerned, too, with how this will affect their emotional wellbeing," she explained.

"I've thought about separating from my husband for quite some time, but I can't swing it financially."

"There are programs that will help you, Mrs. Drake, but no one is telling you to leave your husband. I don't like to see families destroyed unless there is no other option."

"My husband and I were separated a couple of years ago. No, the truth is the girls, and I went to a shelter. I eventually went back to my husband, but shortly after we got back together things fell apart again. I don't see any hope." Farrel knew she'd said more than she intended to, but after she'd poured out her heart to Betty Levitt earlier, she just didn't care anymore. She was tired and emotionally drained. She no longer had the desire to protect Robert. She'd been wrong to do it for all these years. If she hadn't, then maybe he wouldn't have gotten to this stage.

Maggie Browning flipped through a folder. "Your daughters have a beautiful record. They are well-liked and above average students."

"I'm grateful for that," Farrel said. "I was concerned when Charly received detention."

"That was nothing serious. I spoke with Miss Wymer,

and she assured me that Charly is an excellent student. Each teacher develops his or her own form of discipline concerning homework assignments. This is her way of making sure the assignments are handed in."

"My husband gave Charly an unfair punishment."

"I'm sorry to hear that, Mrs. Drake. I do wish, though, that Bobby had as much self-control as your daughters do."

Farrel's eyes widened. "I was not aware that Bobby had any problems in school."

Now it was Maggie Browning's turn to be surprised. "You don't know the problems we've been having with him?"

Farrel shook her head. "No one from the school ever contacted me."

The counselor shuffled through her file. "I see here that we have Bobby's father's work number as our contact number. No home phone number is listed."

"I don't believe this!"

"I don't know what to say, Mrs. Drake. According to your stepson's record, your husband has been very uncooperative."

"I'm not surprised. Robert doesn't take criticism of his son too well."

"I see that Bobby has trouble controlling his temper. How are things with him at home?"

Farrel sighed. "I've always had a loving mother-son relationship with him when I'm alone with him. And Bobby, me, and the girls have always gotten along great together. But the minute my husband enters the picture, Bobby does a complete turnabout. He becomes nasty and cruel."

"Please let me know if I can assist you in any way, Mrs. Drake. And please rest assured, your daughters are very lovely young ladies. You have every right to be proud of them."

"Thank you, Mrs. Browning."

<<<>>>

"Hi, Mom. Need any help?" Charly asked as she came bouncing into the kitchen.

Farrel noted her upbeat mood. It seemed unusual for someone who'd just returned from detention. "You can set the table, honey."

"Okay." Charly hummed as she set out the plates, silverware, and glasses. "What are we having?"

"Stew," her mother answered as she stirred the pot. "Did you see Frankie?"

"Yeah, she stayed after to work on her history report. Remember? She told you this morning."

"Right, it slipped my mind." She turned toward her daughter. Charly was glowing. She couldn't control her curiosity any longer. "Okay, what happened?"

Charly gave her an impish grin. "What do you mean?"

"Your mood. Something terribly exciting must have happened in school today."

Charly walked over to her mother. "I met the greatest guy in the world today." Her eyes sparkled.

"Is he someone new in town?"

"Yeah. His name's Morrison Zaker."

Farrel's lips curved into a smile. She hadn't seen Charly this happy in months. "So, how did you two meet? Give me all the details."

Charly grinned. "He's in most of my classes. I sort of showed him around. He's from California."

"I hope you warned him about our winters around here. He might be in for quite a shock."

"I told him it gets pretty bad sometimes, but he wants to learn how to ski and ice skate."

"*Who* wants to learn how to ski and ice skate?" Frankie asked as she slipped off her jacket and hung it on the hook.

"Morrison Zaker," Charly answered. "He's new in school."

"His sister Lisa is in some of my classes. She's real nice. I told her maybe this weekend we can get together and I can show her around town."

"That would be nice, honey," Farrel said. She glanced at the clock. "Do either of you know where Bobby is?"

"Uh-uh," Frankie said.

"I didn't see him at all today," Charly answered. "Did he even go to school?"

"Well, let's get the food on the table. I don't know where Robert is either. We'll just start without them."

Frankie lifted an eyebrow. "Aren't you afraid of what Robert will say?" she asked.

Farrel looked confidently at her first-born. "Not anymore, I'm not."

The girls looked at each other and smiled.

Farrel was tempted to tell them about her meeting with Maggie Browning but decided against it. There was no need. She wanted them to feel free to speak about their feelings to Mrs. Browning, and they might feel restricted and lose their trust in their counselor if Farrel told them. It was best for them to have someone to express their feelings to. They needed to build trust in adults again. She knew she needed that as much as they did, and maybe even more. It felt good to finally have a friend. This time Robert wouldn't ruin her friendship. Betty Levitt was like a breath of fresh air.

"Let's eat," Farrel said as she seated herself. "Charly, would you say grace?"

"Sure, Mom."

They bowed their heads as Charly asked for the blessing on their meal.

"Real nice!" Robert's booming voice shattered their peacefulness. "Couldn't wait for me and my son! What a way to treat your husband." He slammed his fist on the table, causing some peas to fall out of the bowl.

CHAPTER SIX

"We eat at six o'clock on the dot, Robert." She stared into his eyes without flinching. "Your rule, remember?"

"Don't play games with me, Farrel! Sit down, son, and eat your dinner." He shot his wife a dirty look as he heaped stew on his plate. "Where's the bread?"

"We have rolls," Farrel answered as she passed them to him.

"I want bread." His voice was threatening.

Farrel ignored him and continued to eat her dinner.

Frankie and Charly looked at each other with surprised expressions on their faces.

"I'll get you some, Dad," Bobby offered.

"No, son. It's the wife's *duty* to take care of her husband."

"That's so outdated," Frankie said, rolling her eyes toward the ceiling.

"What did you say?" Robert asked in a loud voice.

"Why should Mom be expected to wait on you?" She kept an even tone of voice. "Why can't you get your own bread if that's what you want?"

Robert stood up.

"Don't touch her, Robert," Farrel said in a warning voice.

"What?" He leaned toward his wife.

"We're not afraid of you. You're not going to scare or

intimidate us anymore. Lay one finger on me or my daughters ever again, and you can rest assured I will bring every charge imaginable against you." Her voice was calm, and she spoke as though they were having a normal family conversation.

Bobby looked at his father. "Remember what you told me, Dad? Are you going to let any woman talk down to you?"

"No, son, I'm not," Robert answered. "You need help, Farrel. Maybe I should be the one to press charges on you for your violent outbursts. When you viciously come at me, I have every right to defend myself."

Farrel laughed. "Robert, listen to yourself for a minute, and you'll see how ridiculous you sound. You're the one who needs help, but you're too stubborn to seek it. You also need to address your son's behavior before it gets out of hand."

"My son doesn't have any behavioral issues."

Farrel frowned. "That's not what the school says."

Robert's eyes narrowed. "What are you talking about?"

Bobby sat frozen in his chair, and Farrel witnessed the fear that crept into his eyes. She hated putting him in the hot seat, but it was the only way that he could hopefully see that his father wasn't helping him by enabling his bad behavior. "You've covered for him just as your family has covered for you," Farrel said. "You're not helping him, Robert."

"You're crazy! Bobby has never gotten into trouble in school. You're just saying that because your precious Charly is a troublemaker."

She shook her head. "No. You gave the school your work number so I wouldn't know the extent of his behavioral problems."

"You're a liar!" Bobby jumped to his feet with raised fists. "I should punch your lying face in."

"Go ahead, Bobby," Farrel calmly replied as she looked

him squarely in his eyes. "But I hope you're prepared for the consequences if you do. Deep down, you know that striking your stepmother is not a normal reaction to what I say. You should be willing to discuss my concerns without the threat of violence."

The boy shook with rage as his eyes darted back and forth between Farrel and his father. After a few seconds, he looked down at his uneaten dinner, then slammed his chair against the table and stomped out of the room.

"Look at him, Robert. He is the product of your own making." Farrel set her fork down. "You need to get his behavior under control before it's too late."

"It's your fault!" Robert spurted as his body shook with rage.

"It's not, and you know it." Normally Farrel would have cowered with Robert's body's reaction, waiting for a slap, kick, or punch, but all she felt right now was a calmness seeping through her body. She'd stood up to Robert and refused to take any more of his abuse. Pouring her heart out to Betty Levitt and releasing Robert's unnatural control over her made her feel not so alone anymore. "You need to take responsibility for your actions. Whether you do or not is up to you, but let me warn you, as I said earlier, you will never touch me or my daughters again." She took a deep breath. "I'm going to see a counselor, one of my own choosing."

"Don't expect me to go with you!" His voice was sarcastic.

"I don't want you to go with me. I'm going on my own. Then I'm going to make some major changes."

"You won't get a cent from me for your counseling," he cautioned.

"I'm not asking you for any money. I'll figure something out."

<<<>>>

Farrel sat on the edge of Frankie's bed, and her daughters sat on the floor looking up at her expectantly, just as they had when they were small, and she wanted to have a serious talk with them.

"What's going on, Mom?" Frankie asked.

"Are we going to leave Robert?" Charly asked hopefully.

Farrel inhaled deeply and slowly let her breath out before answering. "I can't kid myself any longer. You girls know the things Robert has said and done. I'm going to be seeing a counselor."

"We know that, Mom," Frankie said. "You said that at dinner."

"I know, just let me finish." She smiled. "It won't be easy, and we'll have to cut back, but I'm going to check out our options and see what help is available out there. I won't put you two through any more of this abuse. I'm sorry you had to go through what you did." Tears filled her eyes. "I wanted so much more for you two."

"You're a good mom," Charly said. "We don't blame you for what Robert does."

"Mom, you've always spent time with us and talked to us about whatever was bothering us. But mostly you've protected us," Frankie replied.

Both girls got up and put their arms around her.

Farrel dabbed at her eyes. "I don't know what I ever did to deserve you two," she sniffed. "I love you both so much."

"We love you, too, Mom," they replied.

Farrel cleared her throat as her emotions overwhelmed her. "Charly, tell Karla she's welcome in our home whenever she wants to come over, and Robert's punishment is suspended. The school detention is enough."

Charly grinned. "Thanks, Mom."

"I want you both to realize things won't be easy, but we'll make it. We'll still have to live with Robert for a while, though, just until I can put my plans in motion."

Frankie's eyes clouded.

"Before you even think it, Frankie, no, this time, I won't allow Robert to change my mind. I don't care if he does a complete turnaround. I don't trust him anymore, and nothing will change my mind." Her voice was firm.

"Will we stay here or move?" Charly asked.

"I don't know, honey, but it doesn't matter. What does matter is that the three of us will be together and won't have to worry about Robert's mood swings any longer."

<<<>>>

Farrel lay in the darkness, welcoming the chance to free her mind from the long day. She was exhausted but acknowledged the fact that her exhaustion was more from her emotional drain than from any physical labor.

Robert slipped into bed beside her. She felt his breath on her neck when he turned in her direction. Her body went numb. She would not let him try to arouse her. In fact, it would be easy to refute his advances. His touch now made her blood run cold, and there was nothing he could say or do that would ignite a spark.

"What's this?" he whispered as he touched her nightgown. "Let me help you out of it."

"No."

"Come on, babe. We'll work things out. We always do." He caressed her arm. "Playing hard to get?" he teased.

"Leave me alone, Robert." Her voice was firm.

"Look, go to a counselor if it makes you feel better." He leaned over her. "Maybe I'll go with you."

She couldn't see him clearly in the darkness, but she knew he was staring intently at her, assured that he would get his way. "I'm going alone."

"We'll discuss it later. Let me turn the light on low," he said. "I want to look at you."

"No, Robert, I'm tired. It's been a long day, and all I want is sleep."

"I can make you sleep like a baby," he whispered. He moved his hands under her nightgown.

Farrel quickly sat up. "I said no, Robert, and I mean no!"

His body stiffened. "You are my wife, and I expect you to fulfill your wifely duties," he said angrily.

"Maybe I would if you fulfilled your husbandly duties," she retorted.

Robert pulled at her nightgown again.

She slapped his hand away. "I said no, and I mean no!"

"I don't have to beg, Farrel," he snarled. "Our marriage vows include sex."

"They include a lot of things you seem to forget, but they definitely do not include rape!" she hissed.

"Rape by your husband is very hard to prove."

"But it can be proved!"

He sighed. "Come on, baby, let's cut out this nonsense. We're two adults."

"I said no, and I mean no. I'm not letting you manipulate me ever again. Do yourself a favor and get some professional help!"

"Bitch," Robert hissed as he got out of bed and angrily stalked into the living room.

<<<>>>

"What a nice little family gathering," Robert sneered as he walked into the kitchen. He observed Farrel and her daughters sitting around the kitchen table, happily engaged in an animated conversation.

Farrel smiled at her daughters. "This, Robert, is what a normal family is like. But that's something you know nothing about and don't seem to want."

"Give me a break!" He threw his overcoat over the back of his chair. "Where's Bobby?"

"I don't have the slightest idea."

"Why isn't he having his breakfast?"

"I don't know, Robert. Why don't you ask him? I refuse to cater to him any longer. He is disrespectful to me, and I will no longer tolerate his behavior. For years he has seen the way I've allowed you to treat me, so he feels he can also do it. I blame myself for allowing him to think that your behavior was acceptable."

Before Robert could utter a word, Bobby walked into the kitchen, rubbing his eyes. His hair was tousled, and his T-shirt was half tucked into his jeans. "Why didn't anybody wake me?" he snarled. "Now, I'm gonna be late."

"I called you twice," Farrel said calmly. "I'm not going to stand outside your door anymore to make sure you get up. If you don't get up the second time you're called, then you're on your own, pal."

Bobby's eyes widened in surprise. "Are you going to let her talk to me like that, Dad?"

"No, I am not, son." He turned to Farrel. "Apologize."

"You've got to be kidding, Robert. You haven't heard a word I've been saying about Bobby's behavior."

"Never mind, son, she's not worth it," Robert replied as he laid a hand on his son's shoulder. "Sit down and eat your breakfast, then I'll drop you off at school."

"Okay, Dad." He looked distastefully at the platter of

scrambled eggs and sausage. "I want fried eggs and bacon."

Robert looked at Farrel, but she kept her head down as she finished eating her breakfast. "Bobby would like his breakfast." He glanced at his wristwatch. "Come on, Farrel, you're going to make us both late."

"Listen carefully, because I'm only going to say this once." Farrel looked at her husband. "I'm not a maid. From now on, Bobby can eat what's on the table, or he can fix his own."

Robert grabbed his overcoat. "Come on, son, we'll grab something on the way."

<<<>>>

Frankie was grinning when Gary caught up to her.

"What are you so happy about? Or is it because you know you've got the cutest guy on the planet?" he teased.

"Yes, you are the cutest guy on the planet, but that's already an established fact." She smiled as she grabbed his hand. "The reason I'm in such a great mood is because my mom finally stood up to Robert."

"All right! It's about time. What happened?"

"She had a long talk with Charly and me last night. She's going to leave him."

"When?" Gary asked.

"She's not sure. She has to take care of a few things, but at least she's going to do it. That's all that matters, Gary."

"I'm happy for you, Frankie. How about celebrating tonight? No school tomorrow. Remember?"

"Okay. I've got to get to class now, so let me know at lunch what you want to do." She gave him a quick kiss.

<<<>>>

"So, what's on the agenda this long weekend?" Karla asked.

"I don't know. Why don't you come over and we can

think of something to do?" Charly answered.

Karla frowned. "Are you forgetting something?"

She shrugged. "No, I don't think so. Do you have other plans?"

Karla rolled her eyes. "You're not supposed to see me, dummy!"

Charly started to laugh. "I was only putting you on. I know Robert said you're not welcome, but last night my mother ungrounded me and said you can come over whenever you want to."

"Great!" Her eyes narrowed. "But what about the evil one?"

"Forget him. He's history. Mom's dumping him. You should have seen her stand up to him."

"Cool. It's about time." She smiled. "So, Charly, what's the deal with the new guy — Morrison Zaker?"

Charly blushed. "He's so cute. I thought I'd ask him to do something tonight."

"He *is* cute. Maybe sometime you can double with me and Jake."

"I thought you dumped Jake a couple of months ago."

"Oh, I did, but he called me last night. He was so sweet. You should have heard him."

"But I thought you said he ran out on you with Sage Kyle."

She shrugged her shoulders. "He did, but he said she definitely wasn't worth it."

"I hope it works out for you, Karla. After all, I only had to hear about Jake Farmer for two years before you got up the nerve to ask him out in the first place. And he's all you talked about since you broke up."

"I know." She melodramatically put a hand to her brow.

"Love is so fickle."

"I see you've been watching those ancient movies on the late show again," Charly replied and then giggled.

"That's where I learn all my moves." Karla winked.

<<<>>>

Farrel drew a deep breath and then knocked on Betty Levitt's apartment door.

The door was quickly opened. "Why, Farrel, what a surprise. Come on in. I just put on a fresh pot of coffee." She smiled warmly as she ushered Farrel into her bright and cozy kitchen. Farrel admired the homemade curtains and collection of salt and peppershakers.

"I couldn't wait to tell you. I've got some good news," Farrel said. "I've decided to get my life in order. I'm starting by visiting a counselor. I've got an appointment for Monday."

"I'm happy to hear that, Farrel. Good for you." She patted Farrel's hand.

"The talk you and I had made me realize how much I need to unload all of my emotions and put things into perspective."

"Do you know what your plans are?"

"Not really. I'm just going to take things one step at a time."

"You'll make it, Farrel. You're a true survivor."

<<<>>>

Farrel was relieved when she finally reached the tall, old building in the center of town. She hesitated briefly, then slowly opened the heavy door and nervously stepped into the waiting room. After asking her name, a pretty young receptionist said the doctor would see her momentarily. She sat in a comfortable chair, and nervously glanced around the room. She was the only patient in the small waiting area, even though there were two doctors listed. Farrel read their names on a large sign hanging over the receptionist's desk. Dr. Jerry Feldon and Dr. Aaron Berger. Her appointment was with Dr. Jerry Feldon.

A door opened next to the receptionist's desk, and she watched as the doctor poked his head out and whispered a few words to the young woman. Farrel took in the doctor's appearance as he opened the door wider. He was short, thin, and a wisp of gray hair adorned the top of his otherwise bald head. His glasses were loosely perched on the edge of his nose. The doctor glanced at her, and she quickly looked away.

"Mrs. Drake, Dr. Feldon will see you now," the receptionist said with a smile.

Farrel's rose and awkwardly made her way to where the doctor still stood by the opened door. He smiled at her as he motioned her into his office and then closed the door behind them.

"Would you like a cup of coffee?" he asked pleasantly as he seated himself behind a cluttered desk.

"No, thank you," she answered as she surveyed the room. "No couch?"

He laughed. "No couch. But I do have some very comfortable chairs," he replied as he motioned for her to take a seat.

Farrel sat in a dark brown leather chair and nervously clasped her hands together to keep them from shaking. She noticed that Dr. Feldon hadn't taken his eyes off her. "Why do you keep staring at me?" she finally asked apprehensively.

"I'm just evaluating you. Are you nervous?"

"Yes," she admitted.

"Why?"

She shrugged. "I guess it's because things seem so out of control in my life."

"Can you explain?"

"My emotions and feelings...I'm drained. I gave so much of myself away that I forgot to save some for myself. And when I tried to get a little back, my husband gave me nothing." She took a deep breath. "I was patient for so long, holding on to the dream that he would change and treat me with love."

"But he didn't?"

"No. All I got back from him was pain and heartache."

"Why didn't you get out of the relationship?"

She looked into his eyes. "Because I was in love with him, and I believed in my wedding vows."

<<<>>>

Jerry Feldon observed Farrel Blake's shaky movements. She sat slightly slouched, and her shoulders were stooped. It was obvious to him that she definitely had lost her self-esteem. She was an attractive woman, but she could use a few additional pounds on her thin frame. "Would you mind if I called you Farrel?" he asked.

She shook her head. "I'd like that."

He smiled. "Now tell me, why have you made this appointment to see me?"

Farrel clasped her hands tightly together. "As I stated, I'm having problems in my marriage. It can't be saved, and I'm now at a point that I don't want it to be." She paused. "A woman named Mary from the Domestic Violence Center gave me your card. I met her at the hospital one night."

"Mary does good work for the center." He focused his eyes on hers as he leaned back in his chair. "What is your marriage like, Farrel?" He already knew if Mary had talked to her. And, of course, her broken arm was a tell-tale sign, but he needed Farrel to supply the answers to his questions.

"Hell," she answered. "We never should have married."

"Can you elaborate?"

She stood up and walked over to the window. "I thought Robert was the answer to my prayers. I was lonely, and I wanted my two daughters to have a normal life with two parents. My first marriage ended in divorce, and the girls had little contact with their father. I thought Robert would love us and take care of us forever. I was looking for that special magic. Do you know what I mean?"

He saw the pain in her eyes and could almost feel her loneliness. "Yes, I know what you mean." He watched her for a few seconds. "What happened to cause you to want to end your marriage?"

Farrel stared out of the window. "Robert broke my arm. That's when I knew things had to change."

Her voice had dropped so low that Jerry Feldon barely heard her. But he did hear the turmoil in her words. "Did your husband admit it?"

She turned to the doctor. "No. You know, I really thought he would feel bad this time. He'd never done anything this severe before." She threw her hands up in exasperation. "He makes up excuses and twists things around to put the blame on my daughters and me. Robert always comes out unscathed. He is Mr. Perfect." Her voice rose slightly. "He can hurt me how and when he wants, and he doesn't care about the damage to my daughters and me. When he's finished with his verbal and physical abuse, he denies having done anything wrong."

"What are your daughters' names and ages?"

"Frankie is sixteen, and Charly is fourteen," she answered.

"Robert sounds like a very troubled man."

"He is, and I really thought I could change him, but he doesn't want to change." She frowned. "He really needs help," she retorted bitterly. "But he doesn't see it that way."

Feldon was pleased to see she was releasing the pent-up anger, which had taken hold of her emotions. She needed to vindicate herself. He saw that clearly and knew that it would take much time and patience for this woman to fully accept that what had happened to her was not her fault. He sensed that she still blamed herself even though her words said the opposite.

"What made you decide to come to me for help, Farrel? If you want a divorce, then a divorce lawyer would be your better choice."

Farrel's forehead wrinkled. "I deserve a better life. My girls deserve a better life." She wrung her hands. "I don't know what to do to give us that better life."

"Do you think you need to change also, Farrel?"

She nodded. "Yes. I feel so lost. I need to find myself again."

"Do you and your husband argue frequently...daily, once a week, or once a month?"

"We argue almost constantly. No matter what I do, I can never please him." She ran a hand through her hair. "He blames me for all of his problems. He doesn't allow me to have any friends, and I feel as though I'm in prison. He constantly makes fun of me no matter what I do. He picks on Frankie and Charly." A tear slid from her eye.

The doctor scribbled notes as she talked. Robert had taken total control over her life and berated not only her but her children, too. He surmised the damage to her self-esteem went deeper, maybe even deeper than she realized. "Have you and Robert ever separated?"

She lowered her eyes. "The girls and I stayed in a shelter for abused women and children once. I should never have gone back to him, but like a fool, I did."

"Why did you go back, Farrel?"

"He convinced me that it was my fault he abused me."

"Do you have any idea how he could convince you everything was your fault when you knew deep down he'd caused you to leave?"

"I loved him with all of my heart. I wanted him to love me the way I loved him. He said he did, so I went back." She looked into Dr. Feldon's eyes. "I needed him to love me and believe in me."

"Has Robert been previously married?"

"Yes, and he has a son named Bobby. He has full custody."

"How is his relationship with his son?"

She frowned. "It's difficult to put into words. He loves his son, but something is wrong."

"In what way?"

"In his eyes, Bobby is perfect and can do no wrong."

"How does your stepson treat you?"

"With little respect. We used to have a good relationship, but that's been eroded over the years."

Jerry Feldon scribbled some more notes on his legal pad. "You aren't officially separated now, are you?"

"No, but I'm working on it. I finally stood up to Robert and told him if he touches me or the girls again, I'll have him arrested."

"That's good. You should never allow the abuse, Farrel." He glanced at his watch. "I'd like to schedule weekly appointments if that's all right with you."

"I don't have much money," she admitted. "I could barely scrape up the money to pay for today's session."

"Don't worry about it." He smiled. "I base my fees on what you are able to pay. If you can't afford to pay anything,

I'll still see you."

"Thank you."

"Now," he said as he pulled a piece of paper from his desk drawer. He scribbled something on it and then handed it to her. "I would like you to write down how this word makes you feel. It can be as short as one sentence or as long as a filled notebook. I want you to be honest as you express your emotions."

Farrel looked at the word. "Depression," she read.

"I know it probably sounds strange, but I may give you these exercises from time to time."

"Okay."

"Just remember, Farrel, no one has the right to abuse you."

She smiled. "Thank you, Doctor."

<<<>>>

Farrel slipped into the pew next to Robert. Charly, Frankie, and then Bobby followed her. Robert turned and gave her a bright smile. He laid his hand over hers.

Farrel tried to keep her mind on the service, but her thoughts soon wandered. Robert was so loving every Sunday morning when they sat in church together, but the minute they returned home, he became his normal abusive self. Sometimes as she sat in church with her husband and family surrounding her, she prayed something would touch Robert's heart. She hoped he would confess all of his cruel treatment of her and the girls, truly repent, and become the loving, warm husband and step-father that she knew he was capable of being. She turned her head slightly and looked at her husband. Robert turned his head and gave her another brilliant smile as he squeezed her hand.

Farrel turned her attention back to the sermon. Pastor

Walker talked animatedly about evil doings and hidden sins. She wondered how Robert could sit so serenely and every now and then mutter an amen. Didn't he see himself in the message? Didn't he realize he was hiding his own sins? She sighed deeply as she flipped through her Bible to the scripture from which Pastor Walker was now quoting. Through the remainder of the service, she remained wrapped in her own dark, brooding thoughts.

"Nice to see you," Robert greeted several people after the service ended.

Farrel noted how they were polite to her but not as warm as they usually were.

When they reached the exit, Pastor Walker shook Robert's hand heartily, and then greeted the children. When he got to Farrel, he gave her a long, hard look, and then said, "I will be stopping over Monday evening for a visit with you and your family."

Farrel smiled politely, wondering what Robert was up to now.

<<<>>>

"Mom, I'd like you to meet Morrison Zaker," Charly said.

Farrel looked up from the book she was reading. "Hi, Morrison. It's nice to meet you. Charly tells me you just moved here from California."

"It's nice to meet you, too, Mrs. Drake." He smiled. "My father got a promotion, and the move here was part of the package."

Farrel noticed his golden blond hair and bronzed muscular body. "Did Charly warn you about the cold winters here?"

"Yeah, but I'm looking forward to the snow. I only saw snow in the movies or on TV." He grinned. "I can't wait to build my first snowman."

Farrel smiled. "Just don't challenge Charly to a snowball fight," she teased.

"Mom," Charly said, slightly reddening. "Don't give away my secrets."

"First snowfall, and I'll challenge you," Morrison said.

"You're on," Charly replied. "And even though winter's several months away, I won't forget."

"So, what do you two have planned for this evening?" Farrel asked.

"We're going to the movies. Gary and Frankie might go with us," Charly answered.

"Sounds like fun."

"We're gonna go get something to eat," Charly said.

"Okay," Farrel replied. "There's a frozen pizza in the freezer."

Farrel walked into the living room where Gary and Frankie sat on the couch, holding hands.

"Hi, Mom."

"Hi, yourself," she teased. "So, I hear you and Gary are double dating tonight."

"We thought we'd give Charly a break."

Farrel raised her eyebrows in question.

"You know how it is, Mom. It's tough on the first real date."

"It doesn't look to me like Charly's having any trouble," Farrel said.

Frankie laughed. "Well, he is cute."

Gary playfully poked her in the ribs. "Hey!"

"But not cuter than you," Frankie quickly added.

Farrel laughed. "I think I'll read some more."

"What are you going to do tonight, Mom?"

Farrel sensed the worry in her daughter's eyes. "I'm going

to relax for a while and then go back to my writing. I've put it off for far too long."

"What about Robert?"

"I have no idea what time he and Bobby will be home." She patted her daughter's shoulder. "He's not going to hurt us anymore, Frankie. Please stop worrying and have fun tonight."

"I know, but I'll just be glad when Robert doesn't live with us anymore."

Farrel looked at Gary. She picked up on his uneasiness. "I'm sure Frankie's told you what's been going on," she said softly.

"I feel bad for you, Mrs. Drake," he replied awkwardly.

Farrel gave him a warm smile. "I'm just grateful you were there for Frankie, Gary. And I want you to know that I have always trusted you with my daughter."

Gary's face reddened. "Thank you, Mrs. Drake."

<<<>>>

Farrel sat intently writing in a notebook. She jumped when a shadow fell over the page. She instantly looked up. Robert stood smiling down at her. He held a steaming cup of coffee in his hand. "I thought you could use this."

"Thank you." She smiled back at him. "I think my novel is finally coming together."

"What's it about?"

"My life."

"Oh." He pulled up a chair and sat down next to her. "Can I fix you a sandwich or anything?"

"No, thanks." She looked intently at him.

"What?" he asked gently.

She inhaled deeply. "Oh, I was just thinking that it's too bad we can't get along like this all the time."

"But we can. Just give me one more chance," he pleaded. "I promise to make it up to you."

She eyed him warily. "Why is Pastor Walker paying us a visit tomorrow night?"

He hesitated briefly before answering. "He just wants to see how we're getting along. He hasn't been over in a while."

"Okay, I was just curious."

"You don't believe me?" He sounded surprised.

"Robert, I never know what your motives are anymore." She looked down at the steaming cup of coffee. "I wish I could give you what you want, Robert, but I can't. I'm totally drained."

"I could make you feel better," he said in a husky voice as he winked at her.

"Where's Bobby?" she asked.

"At Jimmy Wilbur's house," he answered quickly, taking her question as an acceptance to his proposition. He stood up and reached for her hands.

"What?" she asked with narrowed eyes.

"We have the whole place to ourselves. We just need to get back on track. We never had any problem in the bedroom."

"No, Robert," she said firmly, but almost apologetically. "We had sex, but no love was involved. I see that clearly now. Afterwards you went right back to abusing me. I feel used by you."

"Not this time, babe. I've changed."

She shook her head. "I'm sorry I can't. Not anymore."

His eyes flashed angrily. "You think you're so great, but you're not! Who needs you anyway?" He turned and then stomped out of the room.

CHAPTER SEVEN

Farrel set a plate of cookies on the coffee table. "Would you like some more coffee, Pastor?"

"No, thank you, Farrel." Pastor Walker studied her for a few seconds, then picked up his Bible and quoted a scripture. He looked hard at her. "As a wife, you have certain Godly duties. Many women today do not like the word submission. They tend to feel they are being put down. But God clearly shows us that woman was made for man and man is head of the woman and head of his household. Do you understand?"

Farrel glanced at Robert, who was emphatically nodding his head with every word the pastor spoke. She was seething inside.

"Yes, I understand," she answered. "But God also commanded the husband to love his wife as Jesus so loved the church. And I do not think God said that a man has the right to verbally and physically abuse his wife."

"That's true, Farrel, but we all have our human frailties. I'm sure if you fulfilled your duties as a wife, then Robert would not be frustrated as a husband."

Farrel couldn't believe what she was hearing. "I don't think you have the whole picture, Pastor. I did everything humanly possible to please my husband. I didn't deserve what he did to me. He had no right to abuse me." Her voice was firm. "And he had no right to abuse my daughters."

"Yes, Farrel, but you are missing the whole point. Robert is trying to mold you into the Godly image of the Lord. When you resist him, you just make his job harder. And you set yourself up to face some dire consequences on Judgment Day. Your husband has told me over and over that he has forgiven you for all of your sins."

Farrel turned to Robert. "More lies, Robert?" Her voice was icy. "You can say whatever you like, but you will never convince me that you were ever doing the things you did for God. The God I know and love would never condone what you've done. You should feel proud of yourself."

"Farrel, this is getting us nowhere. As your pastor, I have to listen to both sides objectively. But all I am getting from your side is pent-up hostility toward your husband."

"I'm sorry, Pastor," Robert choked. "I really love my wife, but now you see what I am up against."

Farrel knew the tears in Robert's eyes were just an act. She looked at Pastor Walker, and from the look on his face, it was evident he'd bought into everything Robert had told him. "Pastor Walker, I don't think you can help us. The only hope is if and when Robert decides to tell the truth. Until he does, no one can help us."

"But, Farrel, look at him. He's your husband. He's obviously suffering a deep emotional pain." The pastor slowly shook his head back and forth.

"What about me, Pastor? What about my kids? Who cares about our suffering? I know you saw fresh bruises on my body Sunday after Sunday. You looked the other way. And my arm.... When you asked about it, Robert told you another lie." Her jaw tightened. "Did he tell you how he kept twisting it even though I pleaded with him to stop? Did he tell you how he kept on until he broke it, then refused me medical help until my daughter threatened to call the police?"

Robert sat on the sofa with his hands covering his face. "It's all lies, Pastor Walker, all lies. She needs help!" he moaned. "I don't know how much more I can take."

Pastor Walker stared coldly at her. "Farrel, I can recommend a very good psychiatrist for you. There is no shame. The shame is in not getting the help you obviously need."

"Pastor, don't patronize me. You can talk to my daughters or the neighbors. They'll tell you the truth."

"I've spoken to Bobby, and he said you're always mistreating him and his father," the pastor replied. "Are you calling your stepson a liar, too?"

Farrel laughed hollowly. "What did you expect Bobby to say? He knows what will happen if he tells the truth. Robert rewards him for lying." She threw her hands up in exasperation.

"See what I mean?" Robert said. "Once her anger starts, my boy and I will be in for a terrible night."

"Give me a break, Robert. I'm not angry…just disgusted. All I want to do right now is go to bed and sleep." She looked at Pastor Walker. "I'm seeing a counselor on my own. I'm doing it for myself. I'm doing what I know God wants me to do to protect my daughters and myself. I don't think we have anything further to discuss."

<<<>>>

Jerry Feldon listened intently to Farrel's rendition of the previous evening. "I think you did the only thing you could, Farrel."

"I could have given Pastor Walker the names of people he could contact who could verify Robert's abusive behavior, but I saw no point."

"You seem to be handling it well."

Farrel sighed. "It's not easy. I'm furious to think that Robert would try to get me into bed one night, and the next spread more lies about me. But I know anger isn't the answer. It will only destroy me if I let it."

He was thoughtful for a moment and then asked, "How are your daughters doing?"

"They're calmer since I told them I'm working on a way to be able to financially afford to make it on our own."

"I think you are headed in the right direction. Maybe someday Robert will realize his own need for professional help."

"I don't hate him, Dr. Feldon."

"I know that, Farrel." He smiled warmly. "But sometimes we have to learn to let go of things...or people...who will only harm us."

She nodded. "I know, and that's what I'm doing."

"I gave you an assignment. Did you have a chance to work on it?" Dr. Feldon asked.

"Yes." She removed the papers from her purse and handed them to him. "I think I really got in touch with my emotions over the weekend."

He took the papers and briefly skimmed the neatly typewritten pages. "Would you mind if I read this aloud?" he asked.

She shook her head. "No."

He put on his reading glasses and then began to read slowly.

"Depression, which can be caused by many forms of abuse such as verbal, emotional, mental, or physical, is, in my opinion, one of the most debilitating diseases we humans have in our society. It sneaks up on you when you least expect it and leaves in its path destruction and emptiness. It has no promise, no hope, only failure, and despair. It doesn't happen overnight but creeps out of the day—like a friend embracing you, and only after you are fully enveloped in its warmth do you begin to feel the cold, clammy claws of darkness. It breathes all of your hopes, dreams, and ambitions into its own ugliness, and then leaves you crumbled and alone. No one can reach in and undo the damage. You have to begin the silent battle back into the sunlight. But you wonder if the battle is worth it, for the blackness has convinced you that it is not. You see it in the faces of those you once trusted. The pain squeezes around your heart until you feel you will suffocate from its tight grasp. You retreat into the recesses of your mind where no one can touch you. You long to be like a baby in its mother's womb, protected and safe, but pressures of everyday life invade your security. In the distance, you can see the evil smirk of depression. You want to run, but there is nowhere to hide. Your once safe retreat inside yourself has now also deceived you. You cannot escape. There is no hope. There is only the cold evil pit of darkness waiting to engulf you."

Jerry Feldon removed his glasses and then stared intently at Farrel for a few seconds. "That's very overwhelming," he said. "You poured all of your emotions into this piece."

She nodded slowly.

"Do you still feel this overwhelming sense of emptiness?" he asked, concerned.

"No. Now that I have finally made the decision to leave Robert, I feel reborn, like the chains have been thrown off me." Farrel smiled brightly. "I feel freer than I ever have."

"That's a good start." He glanced at the papers in his hand and then turned his attention to her once again. "Do

114

you write? This doesn't sound like an amateur piece to me."

Farrel's eyes brightened. "I love writing. I always have, but no one has ever taken me seriously...except for my daughters."

"How about Robert? Does he know you enjoy writing?"

"Yes." Her eyes clouded. "He thinks it's a joke. He destroyed some of my work and accused me of wasting money on paper and postage."

The doctor's eyes narrowed. "You have a right to your dreams, Farrel."

"I hope someday it will be more than just a dream. It's all I ever wanted to do." She lowered her eyes. "But almost everyone I've ever known thinks it's a joke."

"What matters, Farrel, is that it's your dream. And from what I've read here, you have a definite gift with words."

"Thank you, Dr. Feldon." She blushed. "That means a lot to me."

"Now I'm going to ask you a series of questions, and you can tell me as much or as little as you like. Due to time restrictions, we will further evaluate your answers in future sessions."

"Okay, but why not do it step by step?" she asked.

"What you tell me today will allow me to review your progress in future sessions. Trust me, I know what I'm doing." He smiled.

Farrel returned his smile. "Okay, I'll do my best."

"Would you mind if I use the tape recorder?"

"I don't mind," she replied.

"Some of my questions may be topics we've already covered."

Farrel's forehead creased. She didn't understand his reasoning, but she liked and trusted Dr. Feldon. "Okay," she said. "I'm ready."

He flicked on the recorder. "Do you blame any outside interference for the problems in your marriage?"

"Yes, I do. Robert's mother constantly belittles my daughters and me. I tried to deal with it, but it's hard to be blamed for things you never did. I wanted to be accepted by her, but she would never allow any closeness between us. She wants Robert to herself. She condones his bad behavior and turns a blind eye."

"Did Robert ever suppress your wants or needs?" he asked.

She frowned. "Yes, Robert could be very selfish at times. He took all of our wedding gift money and spent it on a club membership for himself. After we married, he drained *my* savings but kept his own. He wasn't just selfish with money, but also with his attention and time. Often I felt ignored. And my point of view on any topic was unwanted and disregarded…or ridiculed. The only point of view that he respected was his own or his mother's."

"Did he have trouble adjusting to living with you and your daughters after your marriage?"

Farrel nodded vigorously. "He sure did. He made me feel like a guest in our home and wanted everything done his way. He found fault no matter what I did. The simplest everyday chores, according to Robert, I couldn't do right. He even complained about the way I put the groceries away." She sighed. "He complained every night about my cooking, and I don't know how many times I heard 'My mother cooks it this way, and I will only eat it the way she cooks it.' I always felt like his mother was lurking in the shadows."

Dr. Feldon looked thoughtfully at her. "Did Robert blame you for his problems or for causing them?"

"Yes. No matter what happened during the day at work somehow it was because of me. It made no sense." She sighed again. "He constantly said I needed psychiatric help, and then he'd turn around and say that he was the only one who knew my needs." She frowned. "I shouldn't have put up with it for all these years."

"Did you ever reach a point where you felt it just wasn't worth the battle trying to communicate with him?"

"Yes. I began to isolate myself from him because he totally dominated me. He wouldn't listen to me when I asked him to speak to his mother about her poor treatment of me. I didn't want him to cut off his relationship with her. I only wanted to be accepted and not lied about by her. But Robert always defended his mother and blamed me for her ill treatment. He would say things like I was an unforgiving person. It really hurt me that his mother could say whatever she wanted about me, and I wasn't even allowed the courtesy of defending myself." Farrel's eyebrows narrowed. "He accused me of hating his mother, which I don't. It seemed like his mother was his wife instead of me. I know that sounds odd, but it's the way I felt and still feel. Robert never puts me in the proper priority in his life."

"How were things right after you and your daughters were settled in with him and his son for a while? Did he change immediately, or was it over a period of time?"

"I think it started immediately, only I thought it was just a normal thing couples went through when they were blending their families together and trying to get used to one another. So I didn't think too much about it and assumed after a while we'd all adjust." She cleared her throat.

"But that didn't happen?" Jerry Feldon asked.

Farrel shook her head. "No. He didn't even appear to

want to adjust. Robert spent most of his free time at sporting events with Bobby. When he was home, he would spend hours on the phone with his mother and some young woman who was going through a bad marriage, which was on the verge of divorce. It didn't bother me that he talked with her because the woman was a lifelong friend of his family. I found out later—by his mother's own admission—that she was trying to set him up with this woman. She'd never accepted my daughters and me and never would. It hurt." She blinked rapidly before continuing. "I explained to Robert that he was ignoring my feelings where his mother was concerned, but he accused me of being selfish and trying to control his life."

Jerry Feldon looked at her for a long minute before asking his next question. "So, your husband refused to listen to you or make any changes? Did you admit to yourself that you might have made a mistake by marrying Robert?"

"No. I was stubborn and really wanted my marriage to work. I began to believe that maybe it was my fault, and I should back off a little and give Robert some space."

"What happened?"

She sighed tiredly. "I saw less and less of him. I would look forward to each weekend, hoping to have some time with him so we could do things together with the kids as a family. But he did family things with his son, excluding my girls and me. He never wanted to be alone with me unless it was for sex. I was so lonely." Her eyes filled with tears. "Lonelier than I had ever been in my life. I was so far down on his list of priorities. I came after his personal fun, his mother, his son, his family, his job, and his church obligations. And it crushed me." Her voice faltered. "After a while, I realized that I probably wasn't even on his list."

"Let's take a short break, Farrel," the doctor said as he

clicked off the recorder. "I'll get you a cup of coffee, then we'll continue."

<<<>>>

Farrel held the steaming cup in her hands. She suddenly felt emotionally and mentally exhausted. She hadn't prepared herself for how psychologically draining this would be, going through the recesses of her mind and dredging up all of her painful memories. Jerry Feldon watched her as she sipped at her coffee. Farrel liked him and felt at ease with him. As draining as this session was, it felt good to talk to someone who really listened to her without condemning her.

"Do you want to talk about something else or continue where you left off?" he asked softly.

Farrel took a deep breath, and then let it out slowly. "No, I'd rather continue."

"Okay." He clicked the tape recorder back on.

"I know that I'm probably not making a lot of sense, and my thoughts are disjointed, but there's so much I need to get off my chest."

"It's fine, Farrel. Just say whatever is on your mind."

She took another sip of coffee and then set the cup down. "There are just so many cruel things Robert did to my daughters and me. He would destroy the gifts we gave him. He would say I didn't deserve a card or gift for Valentine's Day, but he would give one to his son and his mother. If I told him I was hurt, he would accuse me of being selfish."

"Did Robert ever complain about your appearance or the way you raised the children?"

She laughed bitterly. "According to Robert, his appearance was perfect, but he always made fun of the way I looked and dressed. He constantly complained about my weight even though I am far from overweight. I could have told him that he was putting on weight, which he was, but I wasn't raised to deliberately hurt someone just to get even. Of course, if I want to be totally honest, I knew the repercussions if I would have said anything to him." She paused. "Robert began spreading rumors that I was an unfit mother, and one time he borrowed money from his mother to get a lawyer so he could get the girls and me out of the apartment." She chewed her bottom lip.

"What happened?" Dr. Feldon asked quietly.

"Nothing. He never went through with it. I did think I had someone on my side who saw what he was doing to me around that time."

"Who was that?"

"His brother. He and his girlfriend treated me decently on the rare occasions I saw them. His brother even tried to have him committed, but his mother intervened."

"Why did his brother want him committed?"

"He witnessed Robert's violent behavior. But his mother said I was the one who brought out the violence in him, so his brother rescinded."

"What kind of reputation does his brother have?"

"I found out that several years ago he was in a rehab because of drug abuse. He never holds a steady job, and consequently, he moves around a lot, owing bills and writing bad checks." She slowly shook her head back and forth. "But he was always kind to me and my daughters."

The doctor nodded as he looked thoughtfully at her. "Did Robert allow you to have anything separate from him, such as a hobby you enjoy doing? Besides your writing?"

"He allowed me to garden. I was surprised but grateful. Each tenant in the building is given a small space to grow flowers or vegetables."

"Did he join you in that?"

"No. But he did forbid me to socialize with any of the tenants."

"He wanted total control of who you associated with, also? Is that what you're saying, Farrel?" Jerry Feldon asked.

She nodded. "It wasn't any better when he was home. I was supposed to devote myself entirely to Robert the minute he walked through the door. He even picked out what TV programs we watched, which were shows that interested him, and I was expected to watch with him even if the program was of no interest to me. If I suggested a program I'd like to watch, he'd refuse. I'd have to sit on the sofa next to him and act like I was interested in the program he chose. I'd long to grab my notebook and write, but I told you how he felt about my writing aspirations."

Dr. Feldon frowned. "Did you ever try to get him to sit down and discuss your concerns like two rational adults?"

"All the time. That's what I've been telling you." Farrel sighed and then helplessly wrung her hands. She was frustrated. Hadn't Dr. Feldon been paying attention to anything she'd said? She didn't know how much clearer she could state what Robert had put her through. "Robert just ignored me when I told him we needed to talk about problems in our marriage. Then, instead of discussing my concerns with me, he would go to his family or co-workers and complain about me not appreciating everything he'd done for me and my daughters." Farrel frowned. "I had to get his permission for anything I wanted to do, but he could do as he pleased when he pleased. Sometimes he would tell me that he wanted to do something special for me and tell me to get ready on a certain date. I would get my hopes up and excitedly wait for the day to arrive, and when it did, he'd pull the rug out from under me and tell me he never planned anything, and that I must have imagined it. He loved making a fool out of me."

"What is your definition of love, Farrel?" the doctor asked abruptly.

Farrel was momentarily thrown off by his question. Her eyebrows drew together, and she was quiet for a long minute. "To me, love does not hurt...it rejoices with truth. Love means wanting to protect the person who is special to you and wanting to make that person happy."

Dr. Feldon nodded. "Do your husband's moods ever suddenly change from calm to explosive?"

"Yes. We can be sitting at the dinner table or watching TV, and he out of the blue accuses me of thinking bad things about him or planning some evil deed against him."

"Do you think Robert spreads lies about you to make himself feel better?"

"I certainly do. He's told me on more than one occasion that he had to defend me to someone. I explained to him he shouldn't have to defend me because I hadn't done anything wrong." She paused and took a sip of her coffee before continuing. "I think he actually wanted me to believe that I was this terrible person so that I would only lean on him. He wanted me to believe that I was unworthy of anyone's friendship or love." Farrel closed her eyes.

<<<>>>

Dr. Feldon sat, watching the young woman. There was so much buried deep inside. It would be a painful process for her to release it, but she would never break the pattern unless she did. "Farrel, tell me one specific event that convinced you that Robert didn't care about your needs." Dr. Feldon studied her facial expression and was surprised that she had an answer so quickly.

"That's easy. My mother's funeral. He refused to comfort me and said that I didn't deserve any sympathy." Her eyes filled with tears. "He accused me of caring more about my mother than him. I couldn't believe it!" A tear fell from her eye. "How could he be so self-centered? He refused to allow me to mourn my mother!"

Jerry Feldon handed her a tissue. "Would you like to stop?" he asked softly.

"No," she sniffed, "I need to get this out."

Feldon wondered how much she would share. She had so much pent up emotions inside of her that he didn't know if she'd pour out everything or bury her true emotions, which she'd obviously been doing for years. He waited until she'd gotten control of herself before asking his next question. "Has Robert ever cheated on you?"

"I don't think so, but I would have no way of knowing." She drew a deep breath. "But he spends a lot of time with an ex-girlfriend. He says they are just friends, but he has never allowed me to meet her."

"Why do you think that is?"

"I don't know. I used to get jealous, but after a while, I just didn't care anymore. I got used to him comforting and showing compassion for everyone else while I had to beg for just one kind word." She slowly shook her head back and forth.

"Does Robert ever show any remorse for what he does to you?" Feldon asked.

"No, he denies doing anything. When he physically abuses me, he calls them accidents because of my supposed clumsiness. It's the same thing when he has a problem, and I try to help him. If I try to give him advice, he tells me I'm stupid and don't know anything. Then he'll go to others for advice. He never thinks my opinion is good enough." Farrel cleared her throat. "Then he'll bring up the submission thing. One time we were on vacation and he made me ride in the back seat for six hours because I couldn't read the road map. He said his son could read the map, so he told him to ride up front. Well, it turned out that Bobby had never read a road map. I told him that I was his wife, and he shouldn't humiliate me in front of the children by making me ride in the back seat, but he said that was where I belonged." Farrel stood up and walked over to the window. "I wish Robert could see what he has done to me. It's easier for me to take the abuse and keep the hurt and pain inside because he always yells at me and calls me a troublemaker if I say anything to him. Robert's mother told Bobby that she would do everything in her power to destroy me." She let her breath out slowly. "I think she's succeeding."

Jerry Feldon stared intently at her. "Is there anything else you'd like to add?"

"I really feel the need to get this out of my system. I've held it in for far too long."

"Just let me know when you want to stop," he said quietly.

She nodded. "Do you remember how it is when you first get to know someone, and you share confidences?" She looked at the doctor.

"Yes," he answered.

Farrel lowered her eyes. "Well, everything I ever told Robert he shared with his mother. I couldn't believe it. It felt like he ripped my heart out. He has no respect for me. My relationship with my husband is unsalvageable. I've gotten to the point where I don't even care to talk to him anymore. What's the point? He's always right, and I'm always wrong. He misinterprets everything I say or my tone of voice, and then he tries to say he knows what I'm thinking. Robert just doesn't want anyone to think anything good about me." She walked back to her chair and sat down. "The more I focus on his manipulation, the more I see what he has done to me. It's like I was blind and now my eyes are finally open." She finished her coffee. "He always justifies his actions and motives. Marriage really means nothing to him. I don't even think that he knows what love is." She inhaled deeply. "I can't stand his lies anymore."

Jerry Feldon watched her carefully as she unburdened her soul. She poured out all of her hurt and anger as each incident entered her mind. He decided to let her continue. She needed this cleansing. It was obvious by the way her face would contort that it was painful for her to relive every humiliating incident, but in the end, he was aware that this was the only way Farrel could begin her healing process in order to become whole again. She had to face her demons head on, or she'd never be whole again.

Farrel's jaw tightened. "Robert had no right to hurt me or my girls. One time he left us with no money, food, or transportation. My support check was late, and I was so scared. I felt like such a failure...he made me feel like a failure. I wanted my girls to have better than what I had been able to give them. I met Robert in the church the girls and I had been attending." She frowned. "I thought since I'd met him in church he'd be the kind of husband and father I was looking for. I dated him for two years. I thought I knew him, but I really never knew him at all." Farrel smiled ruefully. "I used to be so happy and full of life, but now I feel sad and don't see a happy future."

"What was your wedding like, Farrel?" the doctor asked.

She laughed. "You wouldn't believe it. I never got to plan

even one part of it. Robert and his mother made all of the arrangements. I tried to tell him what I would like and that, as the bride, I should have a say in my own wedding, but it made him angry." She quickly blinked her eyes. "He beat me so severely that I had to wear a different dress so no one would see my bruises."

Jerry Feldon sighed heavily. He tried to imagine how anyone could be put through so much abuse and still come out mentally unscathed. And why hadn't she stood up for herself? Before he could ask, Farrel began speaking again.

"My mother didn't attend my wedding."

"Why?"

"I didn't find out until sometime later that Robert's mother had insulted her and said some belittling things about me. My mother thought that under the circumstances, it would be better if she stayed away. She didn't want a confrontation with Robert's mother."

"But you ended up getting hurt."

"Yes. Everyone wants their mother at their wedding. But my mother and I made our peace."

Jerry Feldon leaned back in his seat. "How would you describe your mother-in-law, Farrel?"

"Cold," she stated without hesitation. "She has ice water in her veins."

The pain in her eyes was visible, and from the way Farrel had spoken, Dr. Feldon did not take her statement as being vengeful. The look in her eyes was a testament to the anguish her mother-in-law had caused her. "What you are saying is that no matter what your mother-in-law said, that was the final decision?"

"Yes, her word was the final authority. Like I said, it's like she is Robert's wife, not me. He has his priorities screwed up, and I don't believe he can be committed to anyone because he is always seeking to please his mother and fulfill her desires. He can't seem to break the bond. She has always been in the middle of our marriage bed."

"Do you see much of her?"

"No. I couldn't stand her mistreatment, so I stopped visiting her. I told Robert that I didn't care how much he visits her, but I refuse to go to her house and be mistreated. She talked about me in front of my face while my husband just stood there and said nothing. Then when we got back home, he would accuse me of being rude to *her*."

"Does she visit your home?" he asked.

"Not when I'm there. She told Robert that she would never come to his home if I or the girls were there." She ran her hand through her hair. "I am sick and tired of rejection and being hurt over and over."

"Do you ever feel like you want to get even with Robert and his family for all of the pain they have inflicted upon you?" He eyed her closely.

"No, revenge never solves anything. I'm a Christian, and I receive my comfort from reading my Bible and studying scripture."

He noticed the light that came into her eyes.

"I know that I'll get past all the pain from this relationship, and, realistically, I know that I won't heal overnight, but when I do leave Robert, there will be many obstacles I'll have to face. I've always been a survivor, and I'll weather this storm, too." She smiled.

Dr. Feldon was surprised at her changed attitude. But her last statement showed progress in taking back control of her life. This was the first time she'd actually voiced her resolve to leave her husband. "Do you feel used, Farrel?"

She was silent for a moment and then answered. "Yes, I think I have always felt used by Robert. I know that I was wrong for taking the abuse from him, his son, and his family for all these years, and I take full responsibility for it."

"Before we close this session for today, Farrel, sum up for me what you are feeling right at this moment."

Farrel took a deep breath and then slowly let it out. "Well, I am probably at the lowest point in my life emotionally, but at the highest spiritually. It only takes one person to strip away your very foundation, but I know that the Lord is holding me up now. He is my rock; He is my strength; He is my hope. I can accomplish all of my goals as long as I let Him guide me."

"You spend a lot of time alone, don't you?"

"Yes, but I've finally made a friend in the apartment building I live in. Robert hadn't allowed me to have any friends before." She smiled brightly. "The future used to loom ahead, scary and frightening, and I used to feel so tired and sapped of any energy. But now I have hope. It's amazing what a friend can do."

Jerry Feldon turned off the tape recorder. "We've covered a lot of ground today, Farrel." He smiled warmly at her. "How do you feel reliving all of these emotions?"

"Like a weight has been lifted from my shoulders."

"Good." He stood up. "I'll see you next week, then. But remember, call if you need me for anything."

"Thank you, Dr. Feldon."

<<<>>>

Farrel waited until everyone was seated around the kitchen table before speaking.

"Farrel, this had better be good," Robert warned. "I've only agreed to have this ridiculous meeting to show you and the kids that I'm trying very hard to keep this family together."

"I've got things to do, Dad," Bobby pouted. "I don't see why I have to be here." He glanced at Farrel, then back to his father. "She's probably gonna start it again. Remember what Gramma said?"

"What did your mother say, Robert?" Farrel asked in a calm voice.

"Nothing."

"Robert, this is part of our problem. If you have to hide things from me, then there is no sense in even having this meeting."

His eyes flashed angrily. "Look, my mother sees right through you! You are deliberately trying to get me to lose my temper." His jaw tightened. "It's not going to work, lady! I am the head of this house, and you can shove your meeting!"

Farrel looked at Frankie and Charly, who were quietly listening to the exchange. "Before I met you, Robert, the girls and I had frequent family meetings. It's part of our bonding process."

Bobby snickered. "Gramma's right, Dad, they're a bunch of nuts!"

"I will no longer tolerate you using that tone with me or making fun of me, Bobby," Farrel said sharply. "It ends now."

"Shove it!" he snarled. "I don't have to listen to you."

"You make me sick, Bobby. You are nothing but a wimp who runs to his daddy the same way your father runs to his mommy. Why don't you both grow up?" Charly snapped.

"Do you think you're big enough to make me?" He raised a fist.

"Oh, that's great! I wonder how everyone at school would like to know that you beat up girls," Frankie warned. "You're just like your father!"

"That's enough! You two ungrateful bitches apologize to

my son right now!"

"Don't you dare call my daughters names," Farrel said as she glared at Robert.

"I'll call it as I see it," he answered defiantly. "Now apologize," he said to Frankie and Charly.

Charly laughed. "Apologize to him?" She rolled her eyes and then turned sharply toward her stepfather. "You should be the one to apologize to us for all the unfair punishments and slamming us around!"

"You're a liar!" Robert thundered. "You and your sister need help!"

"Mom, since this is going nowhere, can I please go now? I want to call Morrison and find out what's on for tomorrow."

"Okay, honey." Farrel smiled at her. Charly rose from the table, and as she headed toward the door, Robert grabbed her arm.

"Where do you think you're going? Your month isn't up!"

"Let go of me!"

He squeezed harder. Charly winced.

"Mom!"

"Robert, let go of her!" Farrel demanded.

Robert released her, and Charly ran from the room. He stood as though frozen for a few seconds, and then slowly let his breath out as he fixed his attention on his wife. "How dare you undermine my authority?!" he hissed. He walked over to her and slapped her across the face.

Farrel's hand flew to her burning cheek. She stared contemptuously at him. "I warned you what I would do if you ever touched me again."

"Don't threaten me!"

Frankie ran to her mother's side. "Don't you touch my mother again!"

"She asked for it," Bobby said with a laugh in his voice.

Farrel looked at her stepson and pitied him. Robert would have to live with the consequences of the behavior he'd allowed his son to get away with. She could almost see what Bobby's future would be like, and the abuse that some future woman would undeservedly endure.

"Get out!" Farrel firmly said.

"What?" Robert sneered.

She met his eyes. "You heard me. I've had enough." She took the wedding band from her finger and laid it on the table without taking her eyes from his. "It's over, Robert. I will never, and I repeat never, allow myself or my daughters to ever again live this way."

"Don't you dare threaten me!" His eyes darted back and forth. "You put that ring back on. I'll call Pastor Walker and ask him to come over. He'll calm you down."

"No. I will not attend that church ever again. I don't know what you told Pastor Walker, and I don't care, but I will no longer listen to his twisted preaching again. I will find a new church for the girls and me to attend."

"You need help, Farrel." He looked at Frankie. "You know that your mother needs help, Frankie. Why do you keep defending her?"

Frankie slowly shook her head. "I feel sorry for you, Robert...because you have to live with yourself."

"My dad never had any problems until we met you guys," Bobby said.

"Bobby, deep down, you know that's a lie," Frankie said calmly. "If your father is such a great guy, then why are you so screwed up?"

Bobby raised his fist again.

"Go ahead," Frankie said. "What if I call Gary? Let's see

you raise your fist to him. But you won't. You're just like your father. You only know how to threaten women. It makes you feel good." She stared at him. "But remember, I'm not afraid of you. It only shows what a wimp you really are."

"You wait," Bobby warned. "Someday, you're gonna get it when you least expect it."

Frankie laughed. "I'm shaking."

"Knock it off!" Robert yelled. "See what you've done!" he accused, looking at Farrel. "Now, you've got them fighting."

"No, Robert, you do because you have never taught your son respect for anyone," Farrel answered.

Robert slapped her again, bringing everyone's eyes to his. "Look, I didn't mean to slap you...you just provoked me."

"Like all of the other times? The cuts, scratches, bruises, and broken collar bone?" She looked at her arm. "And this?"

"They were accidents, Farrel. You know that." His voice was calmer now.

"No, Robert, they were acts of violence. Acts that I never should have allowed. I was wrong to have let you hurt me." Tears filled her eyes. "I loved you so much! I thought I could change you. I was wrong because you have to want to change on your own." She looked into his eyes. "I don't hate you, Robert, but I don't love you either. You've destroyed any love I ever felt for you."

"Farrel, we can get through this. I'll change," he said desperately.

"It's the same old promises, Robert."

"I'll do whatever you ask," he pleaded. "Come on...let's talk about it."

"It's too late to talk. Go. I refuse to live with you any longer."

<<<>>>

"So, what happened?" Gary asked.

"I was really scared, but I didn't want Robert to know. He would always feed on our fears, but my mom wasn't scared of him anymore. I was so proud of the way she finally stood up to him." She grabbed Gary's hand. "He packed some suitcases, and he and Bobby left."

"So, what's gonna happen now?"

She smiled. "Mom promised me and Charly that she is finally finished with him."

Gary took a deep breath. "Yeah, but didn't she say that before?"

"I know, but this time she's serious. I know she won't take him back."

"What makes you so certain?" he asked.

"He slapped her again."

Gary's eyes slanted. "Well, I'm glad that I won't have to worry about you with that lunatic anymore." He kissed her cheek.

"I'm just thankful that I had you to lean on."

"You'll always have me, Frankie." He grinned. "Whether you want me or not."

<<<>>>

Morrison smiled. "Sometimes I don't know what is worse—two parents living together and always fighting, or them living apart and me having to be in the middle of their power play."

"Is it really bad?" Charly asked softly.

"It can be at times." He picked up his carton of milk, drained it, and then wiped his mouth with the back of his hand. "My mom started running around with this tennis pro." He shook his head. "But they had problems way before that. Dad wasn't exactly innocent himself." He sighed. "They both tried to get me and Lisa to spy for them on each other. It was hell. Then Dad got this promotion and thought maybe they could put their marriage back together if we moved here, but Mom refused. She didn't even put up a fight for custody."

Charly saw the hurt in his eyes. "Do you hear from her much?"

"Yeah, she's good about writing every week, and Lisa and I might fly out next Christmas."

"I'll miss you."

He looked into her eyes. "I really like you, Charly. You're different from the girls in California."

"How?"

"I don't know — they're kinda phony. I mean, it's like you don't really get to know anything about anyone. People that I hung out with were so shallow. This one girl I thought was my girl, and the next night she was with someone else."

"I hate when people do that," Charly said. "If I'm with someone, I don't look at another guy. Both people should know when the relationship is over. I had a guy who dumped me once, and I didn't even know I was dumped until the next day in school."

"I don't know why anyone would dump you, Charly. You're fun to be with, and very pretty."

Charly blushed. "Thanks." She smiled up at him. "There's something I've been wanting to ask you, but I don't want you to be mad at me."

"What?"

She smiled sheepishly. "How did you get the name Morrison?"

"My parents were kinda like '70s hippies, and a Jim Morrison song happened to be playing on their tape deck the night I was conceived." His face reddened. "Even though it was 1977, they were still in the sixties." He laughed.

"You're a year older than me?"

"Yeah, I got held back a year in eighth grade. That was a rough year." He frowned. "My parents were fighting constantly, and it was hard to concentrate in school, so I sorta bombed out that year."

"I'm glad you did, or I might not have met you."

He took her hand in his as he looked deep into her eyes. "I definitely would have found you, Charly. You're one of a kind. I just like being around you."

She squeezed his hand.

<<<>>>

Mrs. Browning handed Farrel a stack of papers. "If you have any problem getting aid, let me know."

"I just want my girls to be okay through this. I've explained to them that financially, things are going to be tough for a while."

"I'm sure they'll adjust, Mrs. Drake. In my meetings with them, their number one concern has always been for your safety."

"I remember the fun we used to have. We had so many special times together."

"I know you did. The girls told me. You three would take long walks or bike rides, and talk and laugh."

Farrel smiled with the memory. "Charly was always in so many activities. Sometimes it would be pretty hectic scheduling everything, but I wouldn't trade those times for anything. Unfortunately, my husband tried to tear our foundation from under us. He may have shaken it, but my daughters' and my feelings for each other would never let it crumble."

"I can see that," she said. "Nothing can destroy the bond

you and your daughters share."

She looked into Mrs. Browning's caring eyes. "I am worried about Bobby, though."

"He'll be closely watched," she assured Farrel. "His father has been informed of the consequences of Bobby's behavior." She shook her head. "It's a sad situation because his father refuses to believe any allegations about his son."

"I know. I've tried to talk to Bobby, but my husband accused me of picking on him."

"Well, Mrs. Drake, I wish you luck, and I'm sure that your daughters are going to be much happier. I can already see the peace in them."

"I can, too." She stood up. "Thank you for all of your help, Mrs. Browning."

"You're welcome. Just remember, I'm here if ever you need someone to talk to."

<<<>>>

Jerry Feldon observed Farrel closely. "Tell me what you're feeling, Farrel."

She inhaled deeply. "Excited, scared, happy, sad—all sorts of emotions all jumbled together."

"That's to be expected." He looked at her hard. "How are you and the girls adjusting?"

"Good." She smiled brightly. "We may be poor, but we are having so much fun together. It feels great to do what we want to without having to look over our shoulders in fear." Her voice grew serious. "And it feels great not to be someone's punching bag."

"Even though you've had a bad marriage, Farrel, usually both parties still hurt when the divorce actually becomes a reality. It is easy to feel like a failure, and after several months, convince yourself that maybe you should give him another chance. I know that your self-esteem has improved, but Robert has a way of talking his way back into your good graces from all that you've told me."

She shook her head firmly. "Not this time. My girls mean too much to me. If I let Robert back into our lives, they would lose all respect for me."

"What about the lonely nights?"

"I have my writing, and I'm determined to succeed. The girls are very encouraging to me, and they read and edit my material. I like my space and my freedom." She stared into his kind eyes. "Sometimes, I feel the loneliness of not having someone beside me at night, but I quickly remind myself of what Robert has done to me and my daughters."

He studied her appearance. She was wearing a pair of jeans and a sweatshirt. Her hair hung loosely around her shoulders. She had the confidence and the drive to make it through just about anything. She was a survivor. He noticed that she seemed to be deep in thought. "What are you thinking about?" he asked.

She shrugged. "I guess that there are a lot of things I really do not understand. It takes two people to make a marriage. They both recite their vows, but it only takes one person to truly honor those same vows. You can't make the other person do his part. Sometimes it's so hard to let go of the pain and hurt that that person can inflict upon you. Your whole sense of worth can be totally destroyed with just a few carelessly spoken words. Marriage is supposed to mean sharing everything, but how can a man who calls himself a Christian tell his wife that he owes her nothing, and when she has to beg for whatever tidbits he throws her, reduces her to feeling like she is the scum of the earth? Robert never fulfilled his husbandly vows. It took me a long time to face that. He felt manly seeing my pain and tears. That made him feel like a man's man. He would throw insult after insult on me until I was a crumbled mass lying there with my heart exposed — wounded and raw."

"You've come a long way, Farrel." His voice was soft.

"It's a good learning experience. I now see how easy it is to become trapped while I slowly let Robert steal away the strongest part of me to fulfill the weakest part of him. I could never feel secure with him again. Sometimes I think his mental abuse was the worst. He was like a vulture waiting for me to let my guard down, and then he would swoop down, hurling more venom than you could ever imagine anyone could ever do. To Robert, this was love." She took a deep breath. "I know that it will take me a long time to undo all the damage he has done, but I'll make it." She flashed him a bright smile.

He smiled back at her. "You amaze me, Farrel. I have no doubt that you'll be okay."

CHAPTER EIGHT

One Year Later

"I'm gonna miss you, Frankie," Gary said as he gave her a bear hug.

"We got through last year," Frankie said, looking up at him.

"Yeah, but it wasn't easy. I lived for vacations!"

"Me, too," she admitted.

His eyes narrowed. "You just stay away from those jocks. I see how they look at you."

She blushed. "Gary, don't you know by now that you're the only guy I want to be with?"

He grinned. "I think I do." He put his hand in his pocket and pulled out a small box. "But just to be certain, I want you to wear this." He nervously cleared his throat as he handed her the box.

She slowly opened it, and then her eyes grew wide.

"Do you like it?" he asked in a low, husky voice.

"Yes," she choked out and then threw her arms around his neck.

"I know that we have to finish college and then get jobs, so this is a pre-engagement ring."

Frankie looked into Gary's eyes. "I love you." Tears filled

her eyes.

He bent his head slightly, and then tenderly met her lips.

<<<>>>

"So, what are we gonna do tonight?" Morrison asked. "A movie?"

"Nah, I'm tired of movies," Charly answered. "Let's just hang out."

"Whatever you want." He grabbed her hand. "Thanks for being there for me through all the messed up stuff in my life."

She frowned. "I should be the one thanking you, Morrison," she answered. "I'm sure your dad will find a job soon. Just think positively."

Morrison blew his breath out. "Yeah, it's just tough with money right now."

She nodded. "I know. We're in the same situation, but it'll work out."

He lifted a skeptical eyebrow. "I guess you're right, but I wish I could help out more."

Charly tried to find something to say to ease Morrison's mind. "You're already working at The Pizza House, and you have school." She patted his hand.

"I know." He shrugged. "Let's quit this depressing topic and talk about something more interesting."

"Like what?" she asked with a toss of her head.

"Like you," he answered.

"You already know everything about me."

"Well, I have a question for you," he said and then smiled widely.

"You know you can ask me anything."

"Okay." He bit his bottom lip. "I'd like to ask you if you'd wear my class ring."

Charly grinned. "Yes."

<<<>>>

Farrel grinned. "I told you I'd succeed. Even when no one else believed in me."

Jerry Feldon returned her smile as he leaned back in his chair. "What's happened to put you in such a great mood?"

She could barely contain her excitement as she fumbled inside her purse. She retrieved a letter, which she thrust at him. "Read this," she said. "I still feel like I'm dreaming."

Feldon took the letter and read it." When he finished, he smiled broadly at her. "Farrel, this is wonderful news!"

"Thank you," Farrel replied. "You should have seen Frankie and Charly when I showed them the letter this morning. I've been waiting so long for this day, even though a part of me thought it was just wishful thinking. Does that make sense?"

"It makes perfect sense," he replied. "This is quite a sum of money. Any special plans?"

She shook her head. "I don't know. I'm still overwhelmed. But I do know one thing, it sure will feel good to be able to support the girls." She thoughtfully tapped her chin. "I might plan a vacation for this summer. The girls are growing up so fast, and this might be our last chance for a while since Frankie's in her last year of high school and will be going to college this fall."

"You've come a long way, Farrel. I truly believe that you can accomplish anything you set your mind to. You just needed to have confidence in yourself."

"You gave me the tools to find myself again. It's amazing how so much good came out of all of Robert's broken promises. I finally feel like a whole person again."

Jerry Feldon looked intently at her. "You only had to find the missing pieces and put yourself back together. And you succeeded, Farrel."

<<<>>>

Farrel walked through the courtyard, swinging a bag of doughnuts in her hand. "Hey, Betty," she called. "Put on the coffee!" She waved to a few women on her way into the building.

Betty Levitt hurried over to her. "I take it you have good news."

"I sure do. I can't wait to tell you all about it."

<<<>>>

Farrel yawned, then stretched, but didn't make a move to get out of bed as the words of a romantic love song played on the alarm clock radio. Normally she would have pressed the snooze button and gone back to sleep for a few more minutes, but the words of the song held her attention as her mind drifted to a beautiful fantasy that had lately taken hold of her. Did she dare give in to it, or should she continue on and forget her foolish daydreams?

The song ended, and she turned off the radio alarm. Farrel got out of bed and walked down the hall to the bathroom, where she splashed cold water on her face. Next, she walked into the kitchen and made a pot of coffee. When it was ready, she poured herself a cup, and then sat down at the kitchen table and stared at the pile of papers she had left there the night before. The stack of papers represented her latest book. Farrel had to have the final draft on her editor's desk in three weeks. She'd make the deadline with no problem, and figured it would only take her a few days to make the final revisions.

She knew she could have slept in since Charly and Frankie had the day off from school, but Farrel liked to work early in the morning while the girls were still asleep, and the apartment was quiet when she could collect her thoughts and work without any distractions. She took a sip of her coffee and began editing her second draft and worked diligently for the next hour, only stopping to pour herself another cup of coffee.

The phone rang, jarring her, and she hurried to answer it before the ringing woke the girls as she wondered who could be calling at such an early hour. "Hello?" Her eyebrows knitted together as she waited for whoever was on the other end of the line to respond. Someone was there because she heard heavy breathing. "Hello," she repeated. When she still received no reply, Farrel said, "Well, I'm sorry, but I don't have time for games. Goodbye."

Farrel had just settled back down to her work when the phone rang again. She got up, walked over to the phone, and picked it up. "Hello," she said with a trace of annoyance in her voice. This time the breathing was faint. When again she received no response, she hung up the phone and clicked on the answering machine.

"Who was that, Mom?" Frankie asked, sauntering into the kitchen.

"I don't know, honey." She looked at her daughter as she sat back down at the table. "Someone playing games, I suppose."

Frankie's eyes narrowed. "It's been happening a lot lately." She seated herself across from her mother.

"It has? Why didn't you mention it to me?" Farrel asked.

Frankie shrugged. "I didn't want to bother you. You have a lot on your mind with the new book and everything."

Farrel was grateful for her daughter's consideration, but at the same time, didn't want either of her daughters to keep something like this from her. She smiled at Frankie. "The next time it happens, tell me about it, okay?" she said softly.

"Is something wrong, Mom?" Frankie asked, concerned. "Do you know who it is?"

"No," Farrel quickly assured her. "Don't worry, Frankie. But if the calls continue, I'll see if we can have a tap put on the line."

"You don't think it's Robert, do you?" Her eyes widened with fear.

She shook her head. "No, I don't think he'll bother us again. Why would he? We've been divorced for over six months, and we haven't heard from him." She hoped that she eased Frankie's mind, but looking into her daughter's eyes, she realized she hadn't.

"I don't know, Mom," Frankie said in a voice tinged with fear. "Don't forget what he said to you after the divorce."

Farrel reached across the table and patted Frankie's hand. "Honey, please don't worry. Robert won't bother us. I promise." She gave her hand a reassuring squeeze. "Now, I want you to put it out of your mind. Your senior year is almost over, and I want you to have fun and enjoy it." She stared into Frankie's dark eyes. "That's an order."

Frankie laughed. "You're right. I think my psych class has made me paranoid. Especially since I used Robert as my case profile."

Farrel returned her laughter. "So, what do you and Charly have on your agenda for today?"

"We're going over to the Zakers' and hang out for a while. Maybe we'll go to the movies tonight."

"Sounds like fun," Farrel answered. "I'll give you some money, and you can get some pizza."

"Thanks, Mom."

"So, where's Charly this morning?"

"She's still sleeping. Give her another four hours," she

added with a laugh as she stood up. "Well, I'm gonna take a shower, then finish my English report."

"Okay, honey."

Farrel settled back down to her task. The second she picked up her pen, the phone rang. She smiled to herself as she heard Charly's message stating that they were unavailable to come to the phone, and listened for the message or an abrupt cut off, but was surprised when neither happened. She waited for the machine to automatically cut off the caller after the allotted time elapsed, and then got up from the table and raced over to the answering machine. She turned up the volume and listened carefully and intently. Only a steady rhythmic breathing came over the line, with no audible background noise.

Farrel decided to put an end to it now. After what Frankie had said, her annoyance was now turning to uneasiness. She quickly dialed the police and told the officer who answered what had happened. After completing the call with the promise that an officer would be sent, she poured herself a third cup of coffee. Farrel wouldn't be able to concentrate on her work until this unwanted caller left her alone, and hopefully, the officer would be able to put a stop to it today. An eerie chill ran down her spine as she walked back to the table and sat down. What if Frankie was right and it was Robert? Could she really be certain that he was out of her life for good? Or would he keep coming back to torment her? Would she ever be totally free of him?

<<<>>>

Farrel thought back to the last time she had seen him a few days after the divorce was finalized. She was on an early morning jog and didn't notice a car tailing her. Only when she stopped to retie the lace on her running shoe did she notice it, but before she could react, Robert was out of the car and bounding over to her.

Her heart was pounding furiously as she quickly rose. "I have nothing to say to you, Robert," she said coolly.

He smiled warmly at her. "I just wanted to see how you're doing," he said softly. "I miss you, Farrel."

"The girls and I are doing fine," she answered.

"How about a cup of coffee?" he offered.

"No, thank you, Robert," she replied politely, glancing at her wristwatch. "It's getting late. I have to get back."

"Wait...just for a minute."

"What?" she asked sharply.

"Don't you miss me? Even just a little?" He grinned. "Come on...I can tell that you do."

Farrel looked into his dark, brooding eyes. Robert stood self-assured in his typical God's gift to the world stance. "No, I don't. I really don't. I'm enjoying my life, and you need to get on with your own."

"Remember the good times?" he persisted. "We had so many. It wasn't all bad."

"The bad outweighed the good," she said, brushing him off. "Now I really have to go."

"I've changed, Farrel," he pleaded. "I'm asking for one more chance."

"I have no more chances to give you, Robert. It's over. Do yourself and Bobby a favor and move on with your life."

His eyes narrowed and then clouded. How many times had she seen those same eyes change in an instant from affection to pure evil?

"The divorce means nothing, Farrel. In God's eyes, you are still mine." His lips drew into a straight line, and his jaw tightened.

Farrel stood her ground. She wasn't about to be swayed by his phony perception of marriage. "I don't want to hear it. We're divorced. And I know that God understands no matter what you say." She turned to leave.

Robert grabbed her arm. "We need to talk," he said menacingly.

"Let go of me," she said firmly. She was frightened, but she wouldn't let him know that. He played on her fears. No. She'd stand up to him now the same way she had when she'd filed for divorce.

He tightened his grip. "All I want is five minutes of your time."

"I swear I'll have you arrested if you don't let go of me right now," she shouted. She glanced around and saw a couple looking their way. Robert turned his head and spotted them, too. He abruptly released her, and she quickly sprinted away, his threats echoing behind her.

"You'll always be mine! No other man will ever have you, Farrel! Do you hear me?"

She had hurried into the apartment and shakily put the deadbolt on, and then slumped to the floor, trying to steady her breathing. Frankie and Charly ran to her, frantically repeating a phone conversation with Robert.

"He's going to kill you!" Frankie shrieked. "He's nuts!"

"Mom, he said you'll pay for what you've done to him," Charly added in a calmer tone than her sister.

Farrel hugged her daughters close to her. "He's not going to hurt us anymore."

The words were barely out of her mouth when a large crash sounded outside the door. Farrel's heartbeat quickened again as her daughters trembled with fear. A series of thuds on the door followed the crash.

Farrel knew that Robert was on the other side.

"Mom! What are we going to do?" Frankie asked, her eyes wild with fright.

"Go call the police. I'll stay here. Hurry," she whispered.

"Farrel! You belong to me!" Robert yelled. "Open up the door! You have no right to lock me out!"

Charly huddled close to Farrel as Robert continued raving.

Frankie hurried back into the room and sat on the other side of Farrel. "They're on their way," she said in a low voice.

"Farrel! I know you're in there!" Robert continued his barrage against the door. "If you don't open the door, I'll break it down."

"Where are the police?" Frankie was almost hysterical.

"They'll be here, honey," Farrel whispered, her voice barely audible above the hammering on the door.

After what seemed like hours but was in reality only several minutes, they heard muffled voices coming from the other side of the door. The pounding stopped, and Farrel jumped when she heard a loud rap on the door.

"It's the police, Mrs. Drake. Please open the door."

Farrel and the girls scrambled to their feet, and Farrel unlatched the deadbolt and swung the door open.

Robert glared at her before turning his attention to the officer. "This is my wife. She locked me out," he snarled.

"Is that correct, Mrs. Drake?" the officer asked.

She shook her head. "No. We're recently divorced. Robert is not welcome here." She frowned. "I just want him to leave me alone."

Betty Levitt rushed over to Farrel's apartment door and stood next to the police officers. "Are you all right, Farrel?" she asked.

"We will be now that the police are here," Farrel replied.

Betty looked at one of the police officers, "He's not supposed to be in the building."

Farrel watched as the officer motioned to Betty. Betty followed him a few feet away from Robert and began conversing privately with her.

"She's a troublemaker," Robert bellowed, turning his head in Betty's direction. "She has no right interfering in our lives!" He turned back around and stared angrily at Farrel. "I warned you what would happen if you got involved with the neighbors!"

"Please keep quiet, Mr. Drake." The officer's voice was firm.

Farrel looked at the officer. He met her eyes, and she saw compassion in them. She supposed he was used to domestic violence calls. She guessed his age to be early forties. He had a rugged look about him like he spent a lot of time outdoors. His sandy brown hair was neatly groomed, and he wasn't bad looking.

"Do you want to press charges?" he asked Farrel.

She sighed exasperated. "If that's what it'll take to keep him away from us."

"Has he been making threats before today, Mrs. Drake?"

"Yes," Farrel answered. "I've called the police a few times since the divorce. Usually, he just goes away." She explained what had happened on her run.

The officer frowned. "Did you file for an order of protection?"

"No. I never pressed formal charges," Farrel replied in a low voice. She now realized that was a mistake on her part.

He looked squarely at her. "I hope this time you do."

"Got the hots for my wife?" Robert sneered at the officer.

Betty Levitt and the other officer came back in time to hear Robert's question. Betty rolled her eyes as she looked at Robert and then at Farrel. "I'll talk to you later, Farrel."

Farrel nodded.

"No, you won't," Robert said.

"I've heard enough from you," the officer who'd been talking to Farrel said.

"Officer —" Farrel began.

"Officer Haley."

"Officer Haley, I intend to press every charge I can against my former husband."

Robert started to laugh. "Farrel, you can get into serious trouble for bringing false accusations against me."

"Will he be arrested?" Farrel asked as her daughters looked on hopefully.

"When you press charges."

"You aren't going to let him go, are you?" Farrel swallowed hard. She knew what would happen if Robert was set free.

"No. We'll take him down to the station."

Robert's facial muscles twitched, then tightened. "You'll be sorry, Farrel!" he warned as he pointed a finger at her. "You'd better remember to keep looking over your shoulder because when you least expect it, you'll get yours!"

Farrel watched as Robert was read his rights by the other officer and handcuffed.

"Let's go, Drake!" Officer Haley said as he pointed Robert towards the exit.

Farrel saw Betty coming back out of her apartment and hurrying over to her. She gave her a quick hug.

Betty smiled warmly at her. "I'll drive you to the police station, Farrel."

At the station, Farrel looked around the crowded room,

wondering what had brought some of the others to the police station. She observed a woman holding a small baby. The woman was sobbing and pointing to a young disheveled man who was propped against a wall. Apparently, he was intoxicated or high on drugs.

"Here comes Officer Haley," Farrel said in a low voice.

She spent the next hour filling out the complaint against Robert, and then went next door to the courthouse to file for an order of protection.

Robert hadn't bothered her since that day, so she couldn't assume it was him on the other end of the phone now. Why would he start up again? It didn't make sense. She'd just settled down into a happy routine, and now her newfound happiness was being threatened. She wouldn't go through it again.

<<<>>>

Farrel played the tape for the second time.

"How long has this been going on?" Officer Blake asked.

Farrel ran her fingers through her silky hair. "It only happened to me this morning, but my daughter said it has been going on for weeks."

"May I question them?" he asked.

"Sure." She motioned to her daughters, who had been sitting silently at the table.

"When did the calls start?" he asked neither in particular.

Frankie shrugged. "Three, maybe four weeks ago."

"Were they always like this one?" He pointed to the answering machine.

"No," Charly said. "In the beginning, the phone would ring, and one of us would answer it, and whoever was on the other end of the line would just hang up. The breathing started a few days ago."

151

He turned his attention back to Farrel. "Do you have any idea who could be doing this?" He wrote something on his notepad. "A jilted boyfriend?" he probed.

"No, I'm not seeing anyone."

"It's probably Robert," Charly said dryly.

"Who's Robert?" Officer Blake asked.

"My ex-husband," Farrel answered. "I have an order of protection against him."

"Has he harassed you since the order was signed?"

"No, I haven't seen him or heard from him in over a year."

"So, there is no one else you can recall who has a personal vendetta against you?"

"No, I'm only close to a few people."

He snapped the notepad shut. "I'll request a tap, and we'll take it from there. Try not to worry. It may turn out to be just a kid pulling a prank."

"Thank you, Officer Blake."

She showed him out, and then walked over to her daughters, who were standing in the living room, and smiled at them. "Don't you have plans with the Zakers?"

Frankie and Charly glanced at each other and then looked at their mother.

"We thought we might stay home," Frankie said.

"No, I want you to go out and have a good time. I'll be fine."

They eyed her warily.

"I've got to work on the book, then I'll probably have a cup of coffee with Betty and Bill." She hoped her plan helped to ease their minds.

"If anything happens, Mom, you won't hide it from us?" Frankie asked.

"I promise." She smiled at them. "Now go on and have a

good time. That's an order!"

They laughed as they grabbed their jackets and hurried out of the apartment.

Farrel walked back to the kitchen, and for the next few hours, busied herself with the editing. About seven o'clock, she stood up, rubbing her eyes. She stretched, then walked into the bathroom and filled the tub with warm water and fragrant bubble beads. She picked up a popular romance book, and for the next half hour instead of concentrating on the novel, let her imagination take her to an unknown time in the future. A time when maybe she would dare to let romance enter her life again. She closed her eyes and thought about how nice it would be to be truly loved by a man. Not to have to be careful of every word she spoke or be pushed or shoved, but to be treated with respect and talked gently to. She inhaled deeply and smiled. *Dreams do come true*, she thought. Just look at the books. She'd worked hard to fulfill her dream of being an author. It hadn't been easy, but she had always known deep down inside that eventually she would succeed. She was certain she could find true love, but could she ever trust again? Could she ever take that risk again?

She thought about Kyle Haley. Lately, he'd been popping into her mind almost daily. Her heart thumped wildly at the thought of him. He had been so kind to her when she had signed the complaint against Robert. Later that night, he had called her and asked if she'd like to have a cup of coffee with him sometime. She had reluctantly accepted when he called back a few days later. It had been an awkward experience. Part of her wanted to reach out to him, but another part couldn't. She wasn't ready. When she looked at him, her heart pounded, and she realized how easily she could give in to her emotions, so she quickly put the brakes on. She tried her best to explain it to him when he'd asked if he could see her again but knew from the look in his eyes that he didn't buy her explanation. She was attracted to him, but fear held her back. Her heart twisted and then broke. She could never risk betrayal again, even if that meant spending the rest of her life alone. Her mind told her she was making the only decision she could, while her heart was telling her otherwise.

Farrel got out of the tub, toweled herself dry, and then walked into her bedroom. She threw on a T-shirt and a pair of shorts and then ran a comb through her hair before putting on her sandals.

A few minutes later, she was sitting in Bill and Betty Levitt's comfortable living room, sipping a tall glass of lemonade.

"What did the police say?" Bill asked.

Farrel set down her glass. "They're going to put a tap on the line."

"Do you have any idea who it could be?" Betty asked.

Farrel shook her head. "No, but Frankie is convinced that it's Robert."

Betty's eyes narrowed. "Do you think he would dare to start anything after last year?"

"Who knows?" She shrugged. "With Robert, anything is possible."

Betty sighed deeply. "Well, rest assured that Bill and I will keep alert if he comes around." She patted Farrel's hand. "You know you're like a daughter to us."

Farrel's eyes misted. "I don't know how I would have ever made it through without you two."

CHAPTER NINE

Jerry Feldon smiled broadly. "You're looking well, Farrel."

"Thank you." She shifted uneasily from one foot to another as she flashed him a smile.

He hadn't seen her in several months, but her bright, clear eyes and glowing complexion proved that life was almost back on track for her. She had put on some weight, and she carried herself with a newfound self-confidence. Things were going well for her, the doctor thought, but there was something still troubling her.

"Please have a seat," he offered, motioning to the large leather chair near his desk.

"Thanks." She sat down, then cleared her throat but said nothing.

He eyed her carefully. She had come such a long way from the first time he had met her. She was almost full circle, but not quite. There was still an unresolved conflict that needed to be dealt with. "How's the new book coming along?" he finally asked.

"It's finished and with my editor."

"I hope you're going to relax for a while before tackling the next one," he teased.

She smiled. "I still have a few changes to make on this

one. I hope to take a break, but you know how that goes."

He laughed. "I think I know you well enough by now, Farrel, to realize that when an idea pops into your head, a book is soon to follow."

"I'll keep jotting down ideas, but I really am going to take some time to plan a nice trip."

"That sounds exciting. Will the girls be traveling with you?"

"Oh, yes. We're going to have such a wonderful time. I want to spend as much time as I can with them before Frankie starts college in the fall."

"How are they doing?"

"They're both well. Frankie is excited about college and her upcoming high school graduation."

Jerry eyed her warily. "So what's the problem, Farrel? Everything seems to be going well for you, so what's troubling you?"

"I know," she said softly. "Maybe that's it. I had to struggle so hard...it doesn't seem fair."

Jerry leaned back in his chair. "You certainly should know by now that life isn't always fair," he stated. "What's really the matter, Farrel?"

She stood up and walked over to the bookcase, running a finger over the binding of a thick law book then, turning to face her doctor, said, "I've been thinking about Ben Stuart too much lately."

He raised an eyebrow. "Where is that coming from?" Jerry watched as she walked back over to the chair and sat down.

"I don't know," she finally answered with a shrug. "He frustrates me."

"And why is that?"

She took a deep breath, and then slowly exhaled. "I keep thinking about all the years I struggled trying to make ends meet, and how he lived in the lap of luxury. I don't care about myself, but it wasn't fair to Frankie and Charly."

"You never said much about your first marriage. Our sessions revolved around your second marriage."

"Oh, there is still so much to deal with from my first marriage, too," she laughed, with a touch of bitterness in her voice. "Now, if I could only figure out why I involve myself with men who only want to take advantage of me, then hurt me, I might understand myself better."

"Maybe we should take this one step at a time." Feldon caught her eye. "Is Frankie's upcoming graduation causing you concern?"

"Not really...I mean, it just seems like only yesterday she was eight years old. Now she'll be going off to college in a few months. Time flew by, but I've accepted that. I'll miss her, of course, but I have to let her go."

"It's not always easy. She'll be on her own and making her own decisions." He paused. "But she'll be fine, Farrel."

"I know. It's hard letting go."

Jerry smiled. "She's not leaving home yet."

Farrel screwed up her face. "I know. I have several more months with her."

"Is her father coming to her graduation?"

"Oh, of course." She frowned. "Maybe that's part of the problem."

"How do you mean?"

"When I was with Ben, we were your typical young struggling couple. Then when I received some money, we used that to invest in real estate. If it hadn't been for that money, we would never have gotten ahead."

"How long after you received the money did Ben and you break up?"

"Less than a year."

The pain was evident in her eyes. "Didn't you get a fair settlement in your divorce?"

"Yes, the court gave the girls and me enough to live comfortably, but that was not what Ben gave us."

He lifted an eyebrow. "Why didn't you fight it?"

Farrel shook her head. "In the long run, I knew it wouldn't be worth it. Lawyers cost a fortune, and I couldn't afford one. I assumed Ben had a conscience and would realize our struggle and give us the support the court ordered."

"What happened?"

"Nothing. Ben intimated that I should be happy with what *he* deemed I should receive to support the girls. He didn't care." She swallowed hard. "It's not easy to accept the fact that the person you shared your life with and the father of your children could be so cold and uncaring. Especially where the girls were concerned."

"Did Ben ever remarry?"

"Yes, but he didn't have any more children."

"You believe he could have done better by his daughters without being forced to?" Feldon asked.

"Not could have, but should have," she retorted angrily. "A parent should want the best for their children and be willing to sacrifice for them. But not Ben. He was always crying poverty but had a new car almost every year, trips to places he and I had talked about visiting. He had everything!"

"You've kept those feelings buried for a long time, Farrel."

She raised her eyebrows. "That's one of the reasons I became involved with Robert. I wanted to give my girls a better life, and we both know where that got me," she said bitterly. "I went from bad to worse."

"I think it would be good for you to start getting those feelings about your first marriage and Ben out. You need to resolve them."

"I'd love to get rid of all that garbage once and for all. In fact, I thought I had where my relationship with Ben was concerned. Then without warning, something happened to make the old resentful feelings come back." She scowled. "I would just love to move on with my life, and never think about Ben or Robert again."

"And you don't think you can?"

"I suppose not until I exorcise all these ghosts from my past once and for all."

"Tell me what your life was like after your divorce from Ben."

She blew her breath out. "It was one struggle after another. If I paid one bill, I had to let another go." Tears came to her eyes. "There were times I could barely put a meal on the table."

"Did you tell Ben about your finances?"

"Oh, right," she answered resentfully. "If I even broached the subject, he would inform me that if I couldn't take care of the girls, he would." She sighed tiredly. "He loved being in control. If I upset him, he would threaten to cut off the child support completely." She shook her head slowly. "I couldn't win. But I held onto my dream of writing. No matter how bad things got, I knew that no one could take that away from me."

Jerry noticed the light come back into her eyes when she talked about her writing.

"My writing keeps me going," Farrel said.

"How does Ben feel about your book?"

She grinned. "He probably despises it."

"Why would you think that?"

She rolled her eyes. "If you knew Ben Stuart, you wouldn't ask. He does not give compliments."

"Maybe he's jealous of your success," Jerry reasoned. "He no longer can control you financially."

"Could be. I never really thought about it that way."

"Did Ben ever discourage your writing endeavors?"

She shook her head. "No—in fact, he was very supportive. I just don't believe that he ever thought I would succeed. I think he was only patronizing me."

Feldon thoughtfully rubbed his chin as he looked at her. "Farrel, you've got to let go of the past once and for all, and forget what anyone else thinks. You've got a bright, happy future ahead of you. You need to embrace that and live in the present. The past can't be changed…it's gone. Everything that has happened to you has only made you stronger."

"I know," she said uneasily.

"Farrel, you act like you think you aren't deserving of your success. Is that how you feel?"

"No, I worked hard for it."

"Yes, you did." He eyed her carefully. "So, why are you dwelling in the past?"

She sighed. "There's so much I wish I could have done with and for the girls when they were younger." She quickly blinked away her tears. "We were suffering, and no one cared." She looked deep into her therapist's eyes. "Do you know how hard it was to have to juggle finances to give them things they should have normally had?" She didn't wait for a reply. "Everyone else was going on vacations while I was trying to budget school clothes or the next week's groceries. It exhausted me."

"But you made it, Farrel. Look how strong you've

become!"

"I know...and I'm grateful for my success. I just wish it could have come years earlier."

"Farrel, you have a wonderful relationship with your girls. I'm sure that they know the sacrifices you have made most of their lives."

"Yes, they do," she answered. "And I know they appreciate it."

He smiled. "I think you need to get back to planning your trip. Relax...have fun!"

She returned his smile. "I always feel better after I talk to you."

"You've come through some rough times. A lot of women may not have survived the way you have."

Her face reddened. She'd never been comfortable accepting compliments. "You do what you have to do," she said softly. "And my girls are definitely worth it."

"May I offer another piece of advice?" he asked.

"Do I have a choice?" she grinned.

He laughed. "You know me too well. What I wanted to suggest was that maybe it's time you thought about doing something for yourself now that Frankie and Charly are almost raised."

"Such as?"

"Have you thought about dating again?"

A shadow crossed her face. "You remember my last fiasco? The detective?"

"I don't think you were quite ready then. Maybe you could call him or send him a note. He wasn't that bad, was he?"

"No. In fact, he was really kind and gentle. It was my fault. I never gave him a chance." She gripped the arms of her chair. "But I don't think I could call him. It's been a long time. He's probably with someone by now."

"There's only one way to find out," Jerry said.

She sighed. "That would take more courage than I have."

"You have the courage, Farrel." His voice was soft and fatherly. "You need to trust men again. The right one is out there somewhere waiting for you to find him."

Her eyes brightened hopefully.

"You deserve a man who will give you all the tenderness and affection your two husbands couldn't. Take the time to get to know Detective — ?"

"Kyle Haley," she imparted.

"What do you have to lose?" he continued. "If he's not the one, then the right one will show up eventually."

"It's not like I'm going to marry him."

"That's right. Take the time to develop a relationship. Really get to know him. If he tries to control you, then you'll know he's wrong for you. Enjoy yourself! You deserve to have some fun in your life. Explore your horizons."

"It would be so nice to love someone and have that love returned," she said softly.

"It will happen, Farrel, I promise. But you have to take the first step and let down your guard a little."

"I'm going to call Kyle," she said determinedly as she stood up. "After all, what do I have to lose?"

He chuckled.

She looked at him quizzically. "What's so funny?"

"You're like a young girl just discovering the opposite sex."

She winked. "Maybe I am. Only this time, I'm going in with my eyes wide open."

<<<>>>

"So, what are your and Gary's plans for the summer?" Lisa Zaker asked.

"Oh, I don't know." Frankie breathed deeply. "We just want to spend as much time together as we can."

"Are you nervous about college?"

She shrugged. "In a way. It's going to be weird not seeing the same people I grew up with."

"Yeah, I know. But I guess for me it won't be as bad. I had to start over when I came here."

"Do you miss California?" Frankie asked.

"Sometimes." Lisa looked directly into her friend's eyes. "But I mostly miss my mom."

Frankie heard the quiver in Lisa's voice. She looked at her and knew by the way Lisa rapidly blinked that she was fighting back tears. "I'm sure she misses you too, Lisa," she said softly.

"I used to convince myself that she did, and would even make up excuses why she didn't call or write. I wanted so much for her to care about me. I wanted her to be a real mother." The tears brimmed in her eyes and then slowly began to fall, sliding gently down her cheeks. "She doesn't want to know me or anything about me."

Frankie was at a loss for words. She hated the awkward silence and wished that she could think of something to say — anything to ease the pain her friend was feeling. But she stumbled over the words in her mind. She was helpless because nothing she could say would even remotely relate to Lisa's situation. Frankie felt fortunate to have a mother she knew loved her and sacrificed unconditionally for her. She couldn't imagine not having her mother around. But at least Lisa had her father. Eric Zaker genuinely loved his children and did the best he could for them. It was obvious

163

to everyone who met him, and not just an act he put on for public appearances.

"Lisa, if you ever need someone to talk to, I know my mom would be there for you," Frankie said compassionately.

"I know," Lisa sniffed, "and I really appreciate it, Frankie." She wiped her eyes. "I know your mom would talk to me, but I don't want you to think I'm trying to push myself into her life."

Frankie laughed. "I'm not a little kid who's jealous of Mommy."

Lisa smiled. "The best part of moving here was finding a friend like you."

<<<>>>

Morrison Zaker put his hands behind his head and leaned back into the sofa. "So, what did you think of the movie?"

"I liked it. It wasn't what I expected," Charly answered.

"Yeah, it was better than I thought it would be." He put his feet on the coffee table. "So when's Karla Miller moving?"

"In a couple of weeks."

"You gonna miss her?"

Charly shrugged. "I don't know. We're not as close as we used to be."

"It's not because of me, is it?"

"Why would you think that?" She asked with a laugh.

"Well, I take up a lot of your time."

Charly smiled. "That's my choice. But as far as Karla goes, we've grown apart the past year. I'll miss her being around, but it's not like we were hanging out anymore."

"Life's weird, isn't it?"

"Why?"

"I don't know." He frowned. "A couple of years ago, you probably would have been really upset about Karla's move."

"Yeah, we were super close then."

"I just don't understand how people can change their feelings," he said sourly.

"Morrison, people drift apart. Their interests change. All of a sudden, one day, you just realize you don't even like the same things anymore. That's life." She studied his face, wondering what was really bothering him.

"Yeah, like my mom drifting apart from me and Lisa."

Charly heard the anger in his voice. "It's not the same thing. You have a natural bond with a parent. That bond is different than the one you have with a friend."

"Yeah, right," he answered sarcastically. "My bond with my mom is so strong that she couldn't care less if we live or die."

Charly watched as Morrison clenched and unclenched his fists. She wished that she could do something to ease his pain.

<<<>>>

Farrel finished putting the dishes away, then poured herself a cup of coffee. For the past hour, she had rehearsed over and over in her mind what she would say to Kyle Haley.

The phone rang but stopped right before she reached it. *One of the girls must have picked it up,* she thought.

Moments later, Frankie came bursting into the room. "Mom, we just got another one of those prank calls."

"Not again! I'm getting fed up with it."

"I thought the cops were going to put a tap on the line," Frankie said.

"I'll see if Betty can drive me down to the police station tomorrow. We shouldn't have to put up with this!"

"What's going on?" Charly asked as she grabbed a soda from the refrigerator.

"Another call," Frankie answered.

"I'll make sure that something is done tomorrow." Farrel picked up her cup of coffee and walked over to the table. "We've got to start planning your graduation party, Frankie. Is there anything special you'd like?"

"No." She looked at Charly, then both girls burst into laughter.

"What?" Farrel asked, puzzled.

"Nothing," Frankie laughed.

Farrel smiled. "Come on, you two. I know you're up to something."

"It's just that all the kids are having the same party," Charly said.

"What do you mean?"

"Mom, the party will mostly just be a get-together for the adults. Not that I don't want the party, because I do," Frankie explained.

Farrel smiled again. "You're probably right. It's a chance for us proud parents to brag about our children's accomplishments and future goals."

"Well, we'll let you enjoy your day, Mom," Frankie said.

"Oh, I thank you," Farrel joked. "When's Gary getting home from college?"

Frankie's eyes brightened. "In ten days."

"That'll be a relief," Charly said. "At least I won't have to hear her constantly talk about how she misses him."

"You should talk," Frankie said. "Morrison's name pops up about every ten seconds."

"Well, he's going through a tough time right now."

"What's wrong, honey?" Farrel asked.

Charly sighed. "I don't know. He's been thinking about his mother a lot. He's just so depressed."

"Lisa's going through the same thing," Frankie added.

"Is Mrs. Zaker coming to the graduation?" Farrel asked.

"No, she supposedly can't get away from work," Frankie said sarcastically.

"You're kidding! Her own child's graduation? No wonder those kids are upset."

"Lisa never said too much before, but she's so hurt. She was crying, Mom, and I told her if she needed someone to talk to, you would be there for her."

"Of course, Frankie. You know how much I care for her and Morrison."

"Now I know why Morrison is so angry," Charly said. "I didn't know that his mother wasn't coming to Lisa's graduation."

"At least they have a good father to rely on," Farrel said.

"Yeah, but Lisa says there is some stuff you can't talk to your dad about that you would with your mother."

"Tell Lisa I'll help her in any way I can," Farrel said.

"Thanks, Mom." Frankie yawned. "Well, I'm going to bed."

"Me, too," Charly said. "By the way, Mom, call Kyle." She winked at Frankie.

"What?"

"We're not stupid, Mom," Frankie grinned. "We've heard you talking about him to Betty."

"Well, it was just a thought."

"Go for it," Charly urged.

"I don't know," she answered uneasily. "Maybe he's with someone."

"There's only one way to find out," Frankie persisted.

"How do you girls really feel about me dating again?"

"Kyle seems nice. At least what I remember about him. We didn't actually get to know him."

"He's definitely not like Robert or Dad," Charly added.

"I suppose a phone call won't hurt," Farrel reasoned without letting her daughters know that she had already intended to call him.

Charly and Frankie grinned as they walked out of the room.

"Goodnight, girls," Farrel called after them.

She sipped at her coffee for a few minutes and then walked over to the phone and put her trembling hand on it, slowly picking it up. Her palm was sweaty. She took her time pushing the numbers. Her heart pounded, and she could feel her cheeks flush. *This is silly*, she thought. *I'm acting like a teenager.*

The phone rang four times, and Farrel was ready to hang up when she heard the phone being picked up on the other end.

"Hello," a groggy voice answered. Farrel's first reaction was to hang up, but impulsively her hand refused to remove the receiver from her ear. Seconds ticked by.

"Hello," the voice repeated, but now with a trace of annoyance.

"Is this Kyle Haley?" she finally asked.

"Yes, it is. May I ask who's calling?"

"Farrel Drake," she answered softly, almost breathlessly. Her heart was beating so fast that she could barely catch her breath.

After an awkward silence, Kyle spoke. "Is this official business?"

Farrel presumed that he was deliberately putting her on the spot, and she didn't blame him. "No, I.... I wondered if you would like to get together sometime for a cup of coffee." She felt her cheeks grow hot as she nervously toyed with the phone cord. She heard his breath as he slowly exhaled. She was suddenly embarrassed. "I'm sorry, Kyle. I don't know what I was thinking. It's been a year...I shouldn't have called. I'm sorry for bothering you. Goodbye."

She took the phone from her ear, and as she lowered it heard, "Farrel, wait!"

She brought the phone back up to her ear. "Yes?" she half whispered.

"It's not what you think. I'm not with anyone. You just caught me by surprise." His words came in a rush. "If you don't mind, why don't I come over to your place for a cup of coffee? I can be there in twenty minutes. I mean, if right now is okay with you."

"It's fine. I'll see you in a little while."

She hurried down the hall to her room and rummaged through her closet. Finally, she settled for a pair of dress slacks and a simple blouse. She ran a brush through her hair and then walked back into the kitchen and made a fresh pot of coffee. She grabbed a package of cookies from the cupboard and arranged them on a plate. A few minutes later, the doorbell rang. She took a deep nervous breath and slowly let it out, hoping to calm her jangling nerves.

Farrel looked through the peephole and saw Kyle standing outside her door. She took another deep breath, then released the deadbolt and opened the door.

Kyle's muscular body greeted her. He was dressed in a pair of blue jeans and a short-sleeved dress shirt, which had the top two buttons undone.

"It's nice to see you again, Farrel," he said with a smile as he walked into the room.

She returned his smile. "I thought we could have our coffee in the kitchen if you don't mind?"

"That's fine." He followed her into the kitchen.

Farrel poured the coffee and then offered him cookies. An awkward silence fell, and she tried to think of something to say.

Kyle sipped at his coffee as he stared at her and thankfully broke the silence. "I must say that you're looking well."

"Thank you," she blushed. She noticed the rippling muscles in his arms.

"Has Robert left you alone?" he finally asked.

She lifted an eyebrow. "I hope so."

He frowned. "What does that mean?"

Farrel explained about the phone calls. "I can't blame him. It could be anyone."

"But why now?"

"What do you mean?"

"Why would someone just single you out? It doesn't make sense."

She shook her head. "I don't know. Maybe something in my book offended the caller."

"I don't think so. I read your book."

Her eyes widened. "You did?"

"Does that surprise you?" Kyle asked.

She laughed. "It doesn't seem like your type of book."

"You're forgetting something, Farrel."

"What?" she asked.

"I personally know the author. That makes the difference."

Her cheeks grew warm.

"Am I embarrassing you?" he asked.

"Maybe just a little." She picked up a spoon and turned it over. "So, what did you think of it?"

"Hmmm." He leaned back in his chair. "I liked it. It's you."

Her eyes narrowed. "How do you mean?"

"Anyone who knows any little thing about you would know the main character is you."

"Is that good or bad?" she asked skeptically.

"Definitely good. You're a very sensitive, caring person." He stared into her eyes.

Farrel felt like he was staring into her very soul. She wondered what he could see there.

"I think it's Robert," Kyle announced.

"I don't know. The calls come sporadically. It seems odd that he would wait all this time and then start harassing me."

"But just enough to annoy you and upset your life."

She nodded. "I feel like this person, whoever it turns out to be, has the upper hand." She narrowed her eyes. "It's like I'm being watched. I wonder every time I go out the door if the caller is crouching behind some bush, just waiting for the exact moment to make his move."

"Are the police aware of the calls?"

"Yes."

"And?"

"If the calls continue, I'm supposed to notify them, and a tap will be placed on the phone."

"So why don't you have a tap?"

"The calls come in spurts, and since they are considered a nuisance and non-threatening, they decided to wait to see if the calls come more frequently."

Kyle's jaw muscle twitched. "Tomorrow, *you* are getting a tap." His voice was angry and definite. "Are the police aware of your previous trouble with Robert?"

"Yes, but they have no proof that it's him." Farrel twisted her hands together. "At least that's what I was told."

"I'll take care of all the details tomorrow." He reached for

171

a cookie and took a large bite.

Farrel poured more coffee. "Thanks, Kyle, for your help." She looked into his eyes. "But I don't want you to think that's the reason I invited you over."

"Why did you invite me over, Farrel?" He looked intently and expectantly at her.

"The last time we saw each other, it was very awkward, and I felt bad at how it ended. I wanted to apologize." She saw the pain of rejection come into his eyes. It was a pain with which she was very familiar. She had felt that same pain in both of her marriages. She opened her mouth to speak, but before she could utter a syllable, Kyle was on his feet.

"Thanks for the coffee," he said stiffly. "I'd better be going."

She knew that it was his protective instinct. He would never allow her to see his vulnerable side. But she felt the urgency to explain her feelings.

"I'll make sure that you have the tap put on tomorrow," he said indifferently, as though he were in uniform, and she was one of many who called upon him in his role of protector to do the job he was paid for and nothing else. He headed for the door.

"Kyle, please wait." Farrel placed a hand on his arm. She felt the heat of his flesh, and it made her fingertips tingle.

"Farrel, I wish only the best for you, and I'm happy for you that your writing has taken off. You deserve all good things."

She looked up at him until his eyes met hers. "Kyle, will you please just be quiet for a moment and listen to me?" Her voice was louder and firmer than she intended.

He looked deep into her eyes. "What are you trying to tell me?" he asked hopefully.

Instinctively she tilted her head forward, and on tiptoes gently brushed her lips against his.

Kyle was stunned into silence.

"A year ago, I wasn't ready for any type of relationship," Farrel explained, "but I knew that when I was, it was you I wanted to get to know."

A slow grin broke over his face as her words sank in.

"I couldn't stop thinking about you, Kyle, but I knew it wouldn't be fair to you until I had time to get my emotions back on track. I still have a lot to resolve. If you want to take that chance, I'd really like to get to know you."

"Thank you, Farrel," he said softly.

"For what?"

"For giving me something to look forward to again."

Chapter Ten

The jarring of the telephone woke Farrel. She rubbed her eyes and then glanced at the clock on the bedside table. *Who would be calling at 3:15 in the morning*? she wondered. If she wasn't positive that her girls were safely in their beds, she would have become alarmed, but instead, she was annoyed. This intruder was invading her life. It was a game to him. He was in complete control because she had no way of knowing who he was. She could only guess. It was as though the caller knew the moment she found happiness, and then tried to put a damper on it by reminding her that he was still there.

She grabbed for the phone, but the ringing had stopped as quickly as it had started. She lay back against her pillow. Now she knew she would have trouble falling back to sleep. She thought about Kyle and smiled. She didn't know where this relationship would take her, only that she was happy, and that was all that mattered. Nothing had the right to get in the way of her happiness. She'd suffered far too long and had worked too hard to get to where she was today. She wasn't financially secure yet, but with the new book finished, in a year, depending on her public's view of the book, she could be well on her way. And it couldn't come at a better time. Frankie would be finishing her first year of college, and Charly would be planning to enter her senior year of high school. She had dreams for her daughters. Big dreams. But she was realistic enough to know that those dreams could only come true with the best education her daughters could get. And a good education costs money. Farrel wanted to give them the start to a secure future. They deserved that and so much more.

She wished she could turn back the hands of time and keep her daughters close to her for just a little longer. There were so many things she would change if she could, but never the time she had spent with them. That was priceless. Sometimes she worried if that had been enough. Would Frankie and Charlie only remember the bad times when they thought back to their childhood? Would they forget the sacrifices she had made for them, and only remember her mistakes and eventually resent her for them? She had tried to be the best parent she could be, but it wasn't always easy. There had been so many times she had wished for a strong shoulder to lean on. Robert had promised her that shoulder, but then had abruptly pulled it away, leaving her vulnerable and alone. She shook off her depressing thoughts. No. Her daughters would never resent her. The bond she shared with them would never be broken. She had to keep these negative thoughts out of her mind.

Farrel planned to take her relationship with Kyle slowly and with her eyes wide open. She couldn't bear the pain of another failure, and even though the failure of her two marriages was not her fault, she had allowed herself to enter into those marriages. No one had forced her. Farrel wondered how Kyle felt about her two divorces. He'd never said, and she'd never asked. She had to look at his point of view, too. She was a statistic, twice divorced. Kyle didn't appear to be bothered by it, though.

Farrel had no way of knowing the type of men Ben Stuart

and Robert Drake would turn out to be when she entered the relationships with them. She had gone into each of her marriages with confidence and hopes for the future, but no matter what her intentions had been, both marriages had failed miserably and painfully, leaving her wounded and rejected. She'd always been acutely optimistic and believed that somewhere out there was the perfect match for her. Someone who would give her all the tender care and love she had always craved. As the years marched on, though, Farrel had wondered if time was running out for her. Was she getting too old to have these dreams? She knew that she would have no more children. Would that dissuade Kyle? Would he be turned off by the details of her two marriages once that topic came up? Would he somehow misconstrue the facts and blame her? After all, he was a man. Was the saying true that all men stick together? Or was that something some bitter woman had once told her, and it had somehow ingrained itself in her memory? She had to stop it. She wasn't old, and her doubts were ridiculous. Suddenly it dawned on her that she was still terrified to let go and was trying to destroy a budding relationship with Kyle before it even had a chance to begin. It wasn't him at all, but her. Her own doubts would keep her from happiness if she allowed them to take over. Her new self-awareness gave her a lot to think about.

She yawned. She was exhausted but knew that it would be a while before she could get back to sleep. Her mind was too wired. She grabbed her notebook and pen from the bedside table and decided to take advantage of the moment and jot down her feelings and thoughts.

<<<>>>

The morning dawned dark and dreary, and a cool rain was falling. Charly and Frankie sat at the kitchen table finishing breakfast when Farrel, stretching, sauntered into the room.

"Was Kyle here last night?" Charly asked with a sly grin.

Farrel turned to her youngest. "What? No good morning?"

"Just get to the facts," Charly answered jokingly.

"Yes, he came over for a little while." She put a pot of coffee on.

"And...?" Frankie asked impatiently, looking up from her bowl of corn flakes.

"And what?"

"Come on, Mom," Frankie persisted. "We want every detail."

"We're going to try," Farrel replied.

"Try what?" Charly asked with a toss of her head as she rolled her eyes at her sister. "Tell us what happened."

Farrel laughed as she pulled up a chair and sat across from her daughters. "Okay." She propped her chin on a hand. "Kyle and I are going to be seeing each other, but we are going to take things very slow."

The girls smiled at each other.

"But, I want you both to know," she continued, "that your opinion is very important to me. If you pick up on any warning signs that I might miss, please tell me."

"Sure," Frankie agreed. "But he's different, Mom."

"He's not bad looking for an old guy either," Charly added.

Farrel smiled widely. "No, he's not. So, what's on the school agenda today?"

"The seniors are having a rally. Then we get to sign yearbooks and just hang out," Frankie replied.

"Sounds like fun. What about you, Charly?"

She shrugged. "We won't do much in class. Probably just review for finals."

"Do you girls want to do anything special tonight?"

"Sure," Frankie said.

"We could go out to dinner," Charly suggested.

"Okay, you two decide and let me know after school," Farrel said.

Frankie stood up and put her dishes in the sink. "I have to get going. I promised Lisa, I'd meet her."

"Have a good day, honey." Farrel kissed Frankie's cheek.

"Oh, I almost forgot—did the phone ring in the middle of the night?" Frankie asked. "I thought I heard it."

"Yes, but I didn't get to it in time, so I can only assume it was our friend," Farrel said. "But don't you two worry, because Kyle is having a tap put on the phone this morning."

"Good," she said with relief evident in her voice. She picked up her books. "Gotta go."

Farrel poured herself a cup of coffee and then sat back down. She turned her attention to Charly and noticed how tired she looked. "Is everything all right with you, Charly?" she asked, concerned.

"Sure. Why?" Charly looked up and flashed her a weak smile.

"You seem distracted." She patted Charly's hand. "Is there anything you want to talk about?"

Charly frowned and then sighed deeply. "No, everything's fine."

It was a sigh that Farrel knew too well. It meant that life was getting complicated, that too much was happening too fast. Charly was keeping her emotions bottled up. "Talk to me, honey. I know something's troubling you."

Charly sighed again. "Everything's changing, Mom."

"Like what, honey?" she softly asked.

Her eyes narrowed. "Frankie will be going to college

pretty soon, and it'll just be different. That's all."

"She'll be home for vacations," she assured her. "And in the summer."

"It won't be the same."

Farrel gave Charly's hand a gentle squeeze. "I know you're going to miss her, and I am, too. But it's part of growing up, Charly."

"It's not just that." She stared into her mother's eyes. "It's scary thinking about not living all together. Eventually, Frankie and I will be leaving home, and I don't think I'll ever be ready for that day."

"You've got a lot of time before that day comes, Charly." She squeezed her hand again. "Besides, you and Frankie both know that you can live with me for as long as you want. It's going to be hard for me, too, when the both of you leave." She paused. "And believe me, when the day comes that you feel ready to leave, you'll know it and actually be looking forward to it."

"What if something happened to you, Mom, and Frankie and I weren't around?"

"You can't worry about what might happen, honey. We can't predict the future."

"I know, but what if something happened to you while I was still in high school?"

"If by chance, something happens to me, you still have your father."

Charly laughed bitterly. "Yeah, right. He's so critical of everything we do. Nothing ever pleases him."

Farrel didn't know why these dark thoughts were pressing on Charly's mind. "Don't worry. I'm fine. I'm not planning on going anywhere."

Charly stood up. "I guess I'd better get to school."

"Aren't you going with Morrison this morning?"

"No, he had to go early to make up a test."

"Well, don't worry about me. Okay? And don't forget about tonight. We'll have fun." She smiled. "Have a good day, honey."

"Thank you, Mom. I feel better." Charly kissed Farrel's cheek. "See you later."

<<<>>>

Betty Levitt laughed heartily. "You're something, Farrel. I'm happy that you finally took the plunge. Kyle sounds like a nice young man."

"He is." Farrel grinned. "I can't believe that we almost didn't get together because our signals were crossed."

"All that matters is that you did."

"I'm glad he understood why I couldn't get involved last year. But I feel bad that he thought it was because I wasn't interested in him, and didn't realize that I wasn't ready for a man in my life."

"It's going to be exciting getting to know him. You need someone to take care of you." She saw Farrel's eyes narrow, and she put her hand up in protest. "Let me rephrase that. You deserve to have someone treat you the way you deserve to be treated. God knows the suffering you've been through."

"But it made me stronger and better," Farrel admitted.

"That it did," Betty agreed.

"I don't mean to run, but Kyle's coming over. The police finally put the tap on the line this morning, and he wants to check it out."

"Good," Betty said with obvious relief in her voice. "But I still won't rest easy until you find out who the caller is, even though I have my suspicions."

"Let me guess," Farrel said with a sly smile. "Could you

possibly suspect Robert?"

Betty lowered her eyes. "You know perfectly well, Farrel, that I have always suspected him, even though I tried to give him the benefit of the doubt."

"Well, you're not alone in your suspicions. Kyle is convinced that it's Robert, and so are the girls."

"You stick with Kyle, Farrel. My intuition tells me he's the right one for you. And I rarely read people wrong."

Farrel chuckled.

Betty gave her a quick hug. "It does my heart good to see you so happy. Now get going," she said as she opened the door. "And don't forget to give me all the details later!" she called after her.

<<<>>>

Charly was laughing when she caught up to Morrison in the crowded hallway.

He turned. "What's so funny?"

"Stop a minute." She started to smooth his hair into place. "You look like you just stuck your finger in a light socket. Your hair is sticking up all over." She finished patting his hair down.

He laughed as his face reddened. "I'm glad you caught me before I walked into math class."

"It might have destroyed your reputation," she said dramatically.

He laughed again. "I just hope no one saw me."

"So, how was the test?" she asked.

He made a cutting noise as he ran his finger across his throat. "I bombed it."

"It wasn't that hard."

"Maybe yours wasn't, but don't forget, you're the brain in math." He grabbed her arm. "And English, science, French—"

181

She playfully punched his shoulder. "I'm not that brainy."

"Sure," he teased.

"Well, I could tutor you," she offered.

"Didn't we try studying together before?"

"We'll just try harder. You don't want to go to summer school."

He shuddered. "No way!"

They stopped at Charly's locker, where she dropped off a book and picked up two more.

"Hi, guys!" Karla Miller waved. "Wait up!"

Morrison and Charly watched Karla make her way through the crowd.

"I forgot to tell you what I heard this morning," he whispered.

"What?" Charly asked, her curiosity piqued.

"I'll tell you later," he answered as Karla reached them.

"So what have you been up to?" Karla asked neither of them in particular.

"Not too much," Charly replied. "My mom's planning Frankie's graduation party and all that stuff." She closed her locker. "And I've been studying for finals. What about you?"

"I'm getting ready to move."

"When are you leaving?"

"Right after finals."

"Your mom must be upset. She's lived here her whole life."

"So, where you moving to?" Morrison asked.

"Washington."

"D.C.?"

"No, the state," she answered.

"Where?"

"A little town near Seattle."

"Oh." He smiled. "You'll love it there."

"I hope so."

"So, you been seeing anyone special?" Charly asked.

Karla's face reddened. "Sorry, I gotta go," she quickly said as she turned and rushed down the hall, where she soon disappeared into the crowd of students.

"What's with her?" Charly asked as they walked down the corridor. "Does she think she's better than everyone else because she's getting out of this crummy school?"

"That's what I wanted to tell you," Morrison said. "She's pregnant."

"What?" Charly exclaimed, caught completely off guard by his announcement.

Morrison stopped. "Here's my class."

"Morrison, wait!" Charly yelled as he entered the noisy room. She wanted details.

"I can't. If I'm late one more time, I'll get detention. I'll see you after school."

<<<>>>

Farrel knocked on Charly's bedroom door.

"Come in!" Charly called from the other side.

She smiled at her youngest, sprawled out on her bed with books and notebooks strewn around her, and a lopsided stack piled next to the bed. "Busy?"

Charly rolled onto her back and stared up at the ceiling. "Karla's pregnant."

Farrel blinked in surprise. Charly had never been one to beat around the bush. When she had something to say, she just came out with it. But this news shocked Farrel. Charly looked upset and disgusted at the same time.

"I can't believe it," Charly continued. "I know we aren't as close as we used to be, but I still thought she would have confided in me."

"Are you more upset because she's pregnant or because she didn't tell you?" Farrel sat on the edge of the bed.

"Oh, I don't know." Charly looked at her mother. "Both, I guess. It's just stupid!" She punched a pillow. "Karla used to always say that she would never have sex like a lot of the girls in school are doing. Now she's just like them!" she spat out.

Farrel wasn't quite sure what to say, so she sat quietly for a few minutes observing her daughter, silently thanking God that Charly wasn't in the predicament that Karla was. "What did Karla tell you?" she finally asked.

"Nothing. That's just it." She sat up. "She has everyone believing that she's moving and will be going to some fantastic new school."

"She never told you anything? Then how do you know that it's not just some terrible rumor?" Farrel reasoned.

"Because Morrison told me."

Her eyes narrowed. "How did he find out?"

Charly punched the pillow again. "You know how guys are. Supposedly Karla messed around with a few guys. They told Morrison in phys ed."

"Boys tend to brag whether they actually scored or not." She ran her hand lightly over the bedspread. "I wouldn't be too hard on Karla, at least until you know the facts," Farrel cautioned.

"And if it's true?"

"Then she's going to need your friendship more than ever."

"But, Mom," Charly protested. "I don't want her to think that what she did is okay. It wasn't just one guy!" Her jaw tightened. "You should see how some of the girls in school act—like it's a badge of honor. I can see if you made a mistake, but it's still not right. Karla didn't care who she was with, and even if she had only done it once, you would think she would have used some kind of protection."

Farrel sighed. "I know, honey, but I still think you should be nice to her. Who knows? You might just make the difference between her getting her life back on track or her continuing this lifestyle. Think about it."

Charly frowned. "Yeah, but it still makes me mad. I don't even know what to say to her." She chewed her bottom lip. "And how do I bring it up since she doesn't think anyone knows?"

"Just tell her that you heard some rumors and take it from there." She patted Charly's hand. "Come on and get ready. We're going out for dinner, remember?"

"Thanks, Mom."

"For what?"

"For listening."

Farrel smiled. "I'm glad that you confide in me, Charly. It means a lot to me."

<<<>>>

"Need any help, Mom?" Frankie asked.

Farrel grabbed a dishtowel and wiped her hands. "No, I think I have everything under control." Turning to Frankie, she asked with a smile, "Are you all set for graduation tomorrow night?"

"Yes," she grinned. "And especially since Gary is home."

"How'd he do this year?"

"Good. He said it's tough, but he'll make it." She lightly ran her fingers over the countertop. "We're going to go out tonight."

"So, what else is new?" She grinned.

"We won't be late, though, because I have too much to

do tomorrow." Frankie picked up a raw carrot. "So, is Kyle coming to my graduation?"

"No," she answered softly.

"Why?"

"It's not that he doesn't want to," she explained. "We just felt it would be better if he didn't come around this weekend with your father in town."

"So? Dad doesn't have any right to control your life. You don't have to answer to anyone, Mom."

"I know. I don't want anything to ruin your day."

"Dad thinks he's the most important person in the universe." She bit into the carrot. "He just better not say anything to Gary."

"I don't think he will. He has no reason to."

Frankie's face clouded. "He thinks he's right about everything. I can't even talk to him anymore," she said exasperated. "I wish he wasn't coming."

"He loves you and Charly, Frankie," Farrel answered. "Don't ever forget that." Frankie was old enough to set the terms along with her father for the type of relationship they would have now that she was an adult. Ben would have to understand that he could no longer treat her as a child.

"Some help you are," Frankie snapped. "You don't even care about how I feel."

"What did you say?" Farrel asked sharply. "I do care about your feelings."

"You never listened when Charly and I begged you not to marry Robert."

Farrel wondered why Frankie was bringing up the past. Frankie's mood alarmed her. This was totally out of character, and she worried that something else was going on. Tears stung her eyes at her daughter's harsh words. "Frankie, we all make mistakes. I thought I was giving you and Charly a normal family. I didn't know things would turn out as they did. I certainly wouldn't have married Robert if I had known what type of man he really was. But I got us out of it, didn't I?"

"Yeah," Frankie muttered, "but you really have a bad taste in men." Her voice was icy. "We had to go through hell before you left him!"

"What's *really* bothering you, Frankie?"

"Nothing. Just leave me alone." She stomped out of the room.

<<<>>>

"I don't know what to do, Betty," Farrel confided. "I feel like everything is falling apart when it should be coming together." She wrung her hands.

"I wouldn't worry, Farrel. Frankie is an adult now, and she's scared with all the changes about to happen in her life. If she has a problem with her father, then she'll sort it out. Don't be so hard on yourself. I doubt whatever is bothering her has anything to do with you," Betty said softly. "You have a good relationship with your daughters, and you're a good mother."

"It's just so frustrating."

Betty patted her hand. "Did anyone ever say being a parent would be easy?"

"I feel like we're drifting apart." She raised her eyebrows. "I know I'm being overly sensitive."

"You're entering a new phase in your life, too. The girls might have concerns about Kyle, whether warranted or not, because of your past with Robert."

"I suppose you're right," Farrel answered slowly. "I want them to get to know him better."

"Why don't you plan an evening with just the four of you?"

"Things are hectic right now with Frankie's upcoming graduation. I have so much to do."

"Wait until after her graduation, then when things are back to normal," she suggested. "Is Kyle coming to Frankie's party?"

"No."

Betty raised her eyebrows in surprise. "Why?"

"Ben is coming for the weekend."

"Why should that matter? Farrel, when are you going to wake up and quit letting your past rule your future? You made two bad choices with men, but now you have a chance for happiness. What are you so afraid of?"

"I'm not afraid of anything, Betty." Farrel clasped then unclasped her hands. "Maybe I am. Who am I kidding?" She sighed. "I don't want Ben to meet Kyle because Ben puts me down all the time. No matter what I do. But never to my face — he tells the girls."

"Then they have to stand up to him and let him know that they aren't going to tolerate it any longer."

"I know you're right," Farrel agreed. "I'll just be relieved when this weekend is over. I want it to be special for Frankie."

"It will be," her friend assured her. "And I'll be there to help in any way I can" She smiled. "Let's go out to the kitchen. I've got some new recipes I want to copy for you."

<<<>>>

"It's been a long time since I've been here!" Karla exclaimed. "I like your new wallpaper."

"Thanks. So how have you been?" Charly asked.

She shrugged. "I don't know...tired. But I really crammed for finals. At least I passed everything."

188

"Me too. So, when are you leaving?"

"Next week." She plopped onto the bed.

Charly sat next to her. "I feel bad that we drifted apart this year." She looked into Karla's eyes. "I wish we hadn't."

"I know," Karla replied as she directed her gaze away from Charly's penetrating glare. "I guess we just went in different directions. It happens. But I'll always consider you my best friend. I mean that."

"Why?" Charly asked, surprised.

Karla smiled shyly. "Because you're so honest. Some of my new friends only say things they know I want to hear because they don't want to offend me in case they need something from me later. They're shallow."

"So, why do you hang out with them?"

"I wanted to change my image." She laughed bitterly as she lowered her eyes and stared at the print bedspread. "I guess it worked, but not the way I had hoped it would. I just wanted to be cool." She ran her hand over the fabric. "I was stupid," she muttered. "I wish I could change the past, but I can't."

"You'll have a chance to make a fresh start when you move. Just be careful what friends you choose."

Karla shrugged. "I suppose. Sometimes I think I should just stay by myself."

"Don't say that. You'll meet all kinds of new people," Charly said enthusiastically. "Maybe you'll even find a great new boyfriend."

Karla's face contorted. "I don't think so," she said in a low voice. "You're lucky, Charly. Morrison's a great guy." She finally raised her eyes. "I was wondering about something." She chewed her bottom lip.

"What?"

"Have you and Morrison ever had sex?"

Charly's face reddened. "Of course not! I'm not that stupid —" She abruptly caught herself when she saw the ashamed expression come across Karla's face. "I'm sorry, I didn't mean that," she feebly apologized. "I just want to wait."

"Why don't you just tell me you know?" Karla demanded.

"Know what?" Charly decided to play dumb as she waited for Karla's response.

"Charly, quit playing games. You know, or else you wouldn't be apologizing." She looked sharply at Charly. "That's why you asked me over. Do you want to know the details?" Her voice grew chilly.

Charly's eyes narrowed. She was hurt by Karla's response. She'd invited her over because she'd hoped to mend their fractured friendship before Karla moved away. But a part of her was hurt that Karla hadn't confided in her even though they hadn't been as close. She wasn't blaming Karla entirely for the split in their friendship, but she didn't care much for Karla's new friends. As she got more involved with Morrison, Karla had drifted to her new friends. "I don't know what you want me to say." She swallowed hard. "Yes, I know. Why didn't you tell me?" she asked. "Look at all the secrets we've shared through the years. Why couldn't you just tell me instead of letting me find it out from the school gossips?"

Karla started to cry. "Because I didn't want you to think I was a slut and look down on me," she answered in a cracked voice as the tears began to freely flow from her eyes.

Charly hated the fact that Karla had been afraid to confide in her, thinking Charly would judge her harshly. Maybe she had out of shock and anger when she'd heard the news, but now seeing Karla so distressed made her want to comfort her friend. "I would never think that! I just can't believe it happened to you. You always said you were going to wait, too."

"I know," she sniffed. "I was stupid. I didn't think it would happen to me. What did I prove? It certainly didn't make me cool or better liked, except maybe by the guys." She wiped the tears from her cheeks. "And now none of them will even talk to me."

Charly threw an arm around her shoulder. "I'll always be your friend, Karla," she said softly. "You can count on me. I mean it."

"Thanks," she sniffed. "I need my best friend back."

<<<>>>

Gary threw an arm around Frankie's shoulder. "So, are you nervous about tomorrow?"

"Not really. I just don't feel like dealing with my dad all weekend. He gets on my nerves. Nothing I do ever makes him happy. And he never likes anyone I like," she said bitterly."

"At least I'll finally get to meet him."

"That's what I'm afraid of."

Gary laughed. "I'm sure I can handle it."

"You don't know how he is," she said, frustrated. "He can twist the smallest thing anyone says and make it come out bad."

"So, I won't let him." He stroked her bare arm. "You haven't seen him much the past year, have you?"

She shook her head. "No. You'd think he'd be proud of Charly and me and spend the little time we see each other having fun. But no, he has to constantly nag us. The worst part is that he thinks he's perfect."

"Maybe he's jealous," Gary reasoned.

"Of what?"

"I don't know." He shrugged. "Maybe because your mom

got to raise you? Maybe he feels left out of your life."

"It's his own fault that she got to raise us. He's the one who dumped us. He didn't care."

"Well, try not to worry. Tomorrow's your big day. Just relax and forget about what he might say. He might surprise you and not say anything bad."

"It's not easy to relax when just thinking about him makes me angry."

"Is your mom nervous about him coming?"

"I don't think nervous is how she feels. I think she wishes he wasn't coming but feels he should since he's my father. But he dumps on her the same way he does on Charly and me, only not to her face. He waits until he talks to Charly and me." She exhaled loudly. "He gets our whole family upset. I don't know—it's hard to explain." She laid her head against his shoulder.

"It sounds like there's more bothering you," Gary said softly.

"Yeah, there is. I had a fight with my mom. Well, not exactly a fight, but I wasn't very nice to her."

"Why?"

"Because of Dad. That's what I mean. He disrupts our lives."

"I'm sure your mother knows you're under a lot of pressure with your graduation and don't really mean it."

"That's not the point! It's what my dad does. He doesn't even have to be around to cause trouble."

"So? The fight with your mom can't be that bad," he said.

"It was. I said some stuff I shouldn't have."

"Don't worry about it. Your mom's cool. I'm sure she knows deep down you don't mean it."

Frankie squeezed his hand. "How come you always make

me feel better?"

"That's my job," he said, and then grinned. "Now, let's forget all about your dad and think of something else to do."

"Like what?"

"Well, I have a suggestion." He leaned over and tenderly kissed her.

<<<>>>

"Why doesn't my mom care?" Lisa asked, with eyes brimming with fresh tears as she looked into Farrel's eyes.

Farrel gazed into the red-rimmed tear swollen eyes, and her heart broke for the pain this child was suffering. "I wish I could answer that for you, honey," she said softly. "But try to remember how much your father loves you."

"I do, but I miss my mom," she said in a quivering voice. "We're supposed to be sharing these years. She's supposed to want to be with me. A mother just doesn't walk out on her kids." She dabbed at her eyes with a soggy tissue. "Could you just walk out on Frankie and Charly?"

Farrel had to admit that she couldn't, nor could she understand how Mrs. Zaker could have. But she needed to find the right words to make this teenager feel better, not worse. "Sometimes, people make the wrong choices, Lisa. They may feel they are doing something in the best interest of their children when, in reality, it is the worst possible mistake of their lives."

"But I want her to be here for my graduation."

"Did you tell her that?"

"Not in so many words, but she should know."

Farrel frowned. "Lisa, how has your relationship with your mother been since she left?"

She swallowed hard. "Not good."

"Do you talk to her much?"

"Not really. Why should I? She walked out on us."

"Maybe that's part of the problem."

Lisa's eyes grew wide. "Are you taking my mother's side?"

Farrel patted Lisa's hand. "No. I'm not taking anyone's side," she said gently. "I don't know your mother, so I have no way of knowing why she may have left her family."

"What do you mean, then?"

"She might be waiting for you to include her in your life. Maybe you should ask her why she left and hear her reasons. You admitted that you don't talk to her often." She squeezed Lisa's hand. "It could be that she's afraid to ask you to accept her back into your life."

"Why should she be afraid? She's an adult."

"If your conversations with her are tense, she probably feels that you have already rejected her. No one likes to feel rejected, Lisa," she said softly. "Especially by their children."

"Are you trying to tell me that my mom might want me in her life, but she's too scared to tell me because she's afraid I don't want her?"

"It's a possibility," Farrel answered.

"But what if I start being nicer to her when she calls and she still doesn't care? What if deep down, she never cared?" Lisa asked worriedly.

"I doubt that, but even if that's the case, then at least you'll know that you tried."

Lisa's eyes clouded again. "I sort of feel bad that I kept going on and on about graduation and never came right out and asked her to come, or told her that I really wanted her to be there. I expected her to tell me that she planned to come to my graduation." She searched Farrel's face for the answers to her questions. "Do you think that's why she said she had to work and couldn't get off?" she asked hopefully. "Because she thought I didn't want her there?"

"There's only one way to find out," Farrel replied with a smile. "She may have been waiting for you to tell her you wanted her there, but instead, you've been upset because she didn't tell you she'd be there."

Lisa's face fell. "There's no way she'll be able to get here for the ceremony even if she does want to come. She probably wouldn't be able to get a flight."

Farrel was thoughtful for a moment. "If she decides to come and can't get here in time for the ceremony, you can show her the video, and she can at least still see you in cap and gown."

A smile broke across Lisa's face. "I don't have anything to lose," she said brightly.

"No, you don't."

"Thanks, Mrs. Drake."

"You don't have to thank me, Lisa. I only want to see you happy. And you will have a chance to spend some time with her."

Chapter Eleven

"I need to talk to you about something, Kyle," Farrel said.

"I'm not sure I like the sound of that." He sipped his coffee as he eyed her warily. "What's wrong? I was surprised when you asked me to meet you here." Kyle's eyes narrowed. "This isn't like before, is it?"

She patted his hand. "No, I want to apologize again for not including you in Frankie's celebration." She affectionately squeezed his hand. "I really want you there, and Frankie does, too, but Ben can be difficult, and I don't want anything to ruin her day."

"No apology needed. But I intend to be at her college graduation. That is if you can put up with me for that long."

She laughed. "Actually, you're very easy to get along with, and you give me new hope for the future."

"I like the sound of that," he replied and then grinned.

"I need to talk to you about my marriages, Kyle," she said, taking on a serious tone.

"Look, Farrel, that's in the past. You don't need to tell me anything."

"I want everything to be out in the open. Then if you don't want to take this relationship any further, I'll understand," she said anxiously. "But you deserve to know everything."

He looked thoughtfully at her. "I should warn you about

196

something first," he said softly.

"What?"

"After what I already know about Robert, anything you tell me about Ben may just make me want to protect you even more." He took her hand in his. "Because nothing you tell me will ever cause me to love you less."

Tears came to her eyes. "You make me so happy, Kyle," she whispered. "I don't know how I ever deserved someone like you."

"Let's get out of here and go to my place, where we'll have more privacy to talk," he said as he tenderly brushed away the tears beginning to fall from her eyes.

Fifteen minutes later, they sat side by side on the sofa in his small apartment. He took her hands in his and waited for her to speak. She took a deep breath and then slowly let it out. "I don't know where to begin."

"Start at the beginning. Tell me about your family and everything that makes you who you are today."

Farrel drew a deep breath and slowly let it out. "I come from a large family. We're not very close anymore," she explained. "Both of my parents are deceased."

"I'm sorry," he said gently. "When?"

"My father passed away when I was a young child, and my mother died of cancer a few years ago."

"That must have been painful."

"More than you know." She turned to face him. "I was married to Robert at the time. It was horrible! He wouldn't speak to anyone at the funeral home." She closed her eyes for a moment and then popped them back open. "He made a fool out of me and the girls. He sat alone and wouldn't even acknowledge us. Later he accused me of caring more about my mother than I did him. When I tried to grieve, he told me to get on with my life and quit acting like a mama's girl—that's what he used to call me."

Kyle kissed her hands. "I'm so sorry you had to go through that."

"I desperately needed to lean on him during that time. I couldn't believe how cold and heartless he was. It was as though my feelings and pain didn't matter, just so he was happy and in control. His happiness was supposed to be the purpose for my life. He told me that once."

"Farrel, I wish I could have been there for you and the girls during that painful time." He stroked her hair.

"What would you have done?" She searched his face. "Tell me," she whispered.

He brushed his lips against hers. "I would have held you while you cried, and I would have cried with you. Then I would have listened while you talked through your grief."

She looked into his eyes.

"I would have given you both of my shoulders to lean on. And I wouldn't have let you go until I knew you were ready, no matter how long it took."

Farrel rested her head against his chest. "Robert used to tell me he would be there for me, but whenever I needed him, he accused me of making my own problems in my life."

"I would never do that." He stroked her cheek.

She could feel his heart pounding as she closed her eyes. It felt so good to be this close to him. Her own heart was pumping with a new intensity, and she knew that she was feeling the first stirrings of love. She was frightened because as much as she wanted to trust Kyle, she still didn't know if she could fully trust any man again.

"Farrel," he whispered, "I'm not Ben Stuart or Robert Drake."

"I know," she whispered back. "I know." She burrowed deeper into his chest, relishing the security she felt there.

<<<>>>

"Frankie, you look beautiful!" Farrel exclaimed as she proudly snapped a picture of her daughter in cap and gown.

"There's my girl," Ben Stuart beamed as he entered the room. "I'll want copies of all the pictures," he said to Farrel as he continued to look at Frankie.

"Of course," Farrel answered. "Is Gary coming here or meeting us there?" she asked.

"He's going to meet us there." Frankie slowly turned around. "Is everything all right on me?" she asked anxiously.

Farrel kissed her cheek. "Yes, everything is perfect." She stared into her daughter's eyes. "I'm so proud of you."

Frankie gave her a weak smile. "I'll be glad when this is over."

"I guess we'd better get going. Where's Charly?" Farrel asked.

"I'm ready," Charly panted as she hurried into the room. "I was on the phone."

"You'll see Morrison there," her sister said exasperatedly.

"I know, but he's still upset about his mom," she replied sympathetically. "I feel bad for him and Lisa."

"Oh?" Ben arched his eyebrows. "Is there something I should know?"

"We gotta go, Dad," Frankie interrupted.

He picked up his jacket. "I want to talk to you girls about your boyfriends sometime this weekend," he said as he put his jacket on.

"Sure," Charly muttered.

<<<>>>

Farrel's heart swelled with pride as she watched Frankie

199

walk across the stage to accept her diploma. She stole a glance at Ben. His expression didn't give her a clue as to what he was thinking. She thought how nice it would be to have Kyle sitting beside her. He made her feel so alive and filled with hope. But she knew that she had to tread slowly. Her heart couldn't take any more trauma. After the ceremony, she proudly followed Frankie around as she hugged her friends, then posed for pictures with them.

"I didn't know that she was close to anyone," Ben said with a trace of surprise in his voice.

"What did you think she did, Dad? Stay in her room all the time?" Charly asked sarcastically.

"As a matter of fact, I did." He faced Farrel. "When you were with Robert, didn't she isolate herself?"

"That was a long time ago," Farrel answered coolly.

"Yeah," Charly said. "She might be a geek, but she does have friends."

"Charly, that's not nice. She's not a geek," Farrel gently scolded.

Ben stuffed his hands into his pockets as his eyes traveled over the sea of graduates and their guests. Finally, his eyes rested on Frankie and Gary. "Who's that boy with Frankie?"

"Gary the geek," Charly said with a laugh. "Just kidding. He's a cool guy."

"That's the boy she's so infatuated with?"

"He's a nice boy," Farrel quickly defended.

"Hmmm. So why haven't I ever met him?"

"It's not like you've visited here much, Ben. The girls have always flown to your home. You never spent time on their turf."

"She's too young to be tied down." He grunted. "I think college will be good for her. In a few months, Gary will just be a fond memory." His voice was matter-of-fact.

"I don't think so. Frankie and Gary have been together for a long time, and college certainly has not changed his feelings for her," Farrel explained.

Ben shook his head. "She's young—there'll be many boys before she settles down. Mark my words."

Farrel glanced at Charly, who rolled her eyes. They both knew that it would do no good to try to explain anything to Ben Stuart. He was a self-proclaimed expert on any topic—even though he knew nothing about it.

"So, where's this Morrison you're so hung up on?" Ben asked Charly as he looked pointedly at her.

She shrugged. "He said they were leaving right after the ceremony."

"Without even telling you goodbye? That seems odd. I was hoping to meet him."

"Nothing odd about it," Charly countered. "I talked to him before and after the ceremony while you were tagging Mom and Frankie around."

Farrel held her breath, waiting for Ben's reaction, but surprisingly he stood with a surprised look on his face but offered no retort.

"You can meet Morrison tomorrow at Frankie's party," Charly informed her father.

"Am I going to meet Gary, too?"

"Give her a chance, Ben. She'll introduce you when the time is right."

He shook his head again. "I don't know, Farrel. Sometimes I wonder about the way you've raised the girls."

Farrel silently prayed that Ben wouldn't do anything tomorrow to ruin Frankie's party. He had a knack for offending anyone who didn't agree with his narrow-minded viewpoints.

<<<>>>

"Need help?" Betty asked.

Farrel surveyed Frankie's guests, who were mingling around the grill waiting for the hamburgers and hot-dogs. "You can take this tray of vegetables and dips out if you'd like."

"Sure." Betty smiled. "I see you're keeping Ben occupied."

She laughed. "I promised Frankie I'd keep him out of her way as much as possible. So far, so good."

"Looks like it's working." Betty looked around. "You have a nice turnout."

"Better than I thought. I was worried this morning. It looked like rain, and there's no way I could fit everyone into the apartment. I'm happy that the apartment manager allowed us to use this section for the party."

"The manager would have let you use the community building if it had rained."

"I never even thought about that," Farrel said. "My mind's been in a whirl lately."

Betty peered out the window. "Charly seems lost. Where's Morrison?"

"Oh, I forgot to tell you," Farrel said as she wiped her hands on a dishtowel. "He called early this morning. He was so excited. When they got home last night, Mrs. Zaker was waiting for them. I was thrilled for Lisa. Even though her mother's plane arrived too late for the ceremony, at least she did show up. And since the graduation was taped, she got to watch it."

"Are they coming over?"

"They were going to, but Morrison said they have a lot to discuss with their mother. She's planning to take Lisa and

Morrison on a trip this summer to get reacquainted."

"I'm so happy for them," Betty began. "But, I suppose it'll be hard for Charly."

Farrel sighed. "I hope the trip I'm planning for the girls and me will take her mind off him and Frankie's leaving for college this fall. She tries to hide it, but I know she's upset."

"I'm sure she'll be fine." Betty picked up the tray. "But just the same, I'll go see if I can cheer her up. Maybe she's feeling a little left out."

"I've tried to spend time with her, but she's at such a difficult stage." She put some crackers on a plate. "And then the Karla Miller situation hasn't helped."

"Oh, I know!" Betty exclaimed. "I was so shocked. But I think Charly handled that with a great deal of maturity and compassion for Karla."

"That she did," Farrel proudly agreed. "Karla and Charly have been friends for so long, and to be honest, I'm glad they're back on track."

Betty frowned. "I don't want to interfere, Farrel, but I think Kyle should be here. If he's going to be a part of your life, he needs to be included regardless of Ben. After all, Ben has his own life, and I've never heard you say a disparaging word or interfere."

Farrel sighed. "Betty, I want nothing more than to have Kyle with me at this moment. I don't know if I can explain this, but I feel so different when he's around."

Her friend laughed. "I believe it's called love, Farrel."

Her face reddened.

"Give in to it," Betty prodded. "You can't fight it. You've got it bad, girl."

"I've known it for a while," she admitted. "I wanted him with me so desperately last night at the graduation and especially today, but I couldn't let Ben give him the third degree. I've talked to Kyle about it, and he really does understand."

"Think of yourself and your happiness for once, Farrel," Betty said as she opened the door. "Don't let anyone destroy your happiness."

<<<>>>

Later that night, Farrel plopped into a chair, physically exhausted, but pleased with the success of Frankie's party. Everyone appeared to have had a good time, and Ben had even complimented her on how nice it was. She rubbed her eyes, and then looked at the counter and sink, which were brimming with dirty dishes. She groaned as she thought of the dreaded task ahead of her. Slowly she rose, making her way over to the sink and began scraping plates. Her thoughts were on Kyle. She filled the sink with hot, soapy water and then slowly washed a plate. Farrel closed her eyes and fantasized about Kyle's strong hands caressing her shoulders and neck. She felt goosebumps on her tingling flesh. No man had ever made her feel this way before, and she knew it was time to tell Kyle how she really felt about him.

"Hi, Mom."

Farrel opened her eyes, startled by the intrusion.

Charly plopped down into a chair at the kitchen table. Farrel saw the sadness in her daughter's eyes. "Hi, Charly. Did you have fun today?"

She shrugged the typical teenager, *It was okay,* shrug.

"So, how was your talk with your father?"

Charly exhaled loudly. "The same basic conversation. He should just make a tape since he never says anything new. He's right about everything, and I'm wrong about everything."

"Don't let it get to you, honey. You know deep down

inside the real truth."

"Well, he still puts you down!" Her voice was angry. "I don't like it."

"Don't worry about it. Charly. It doesn't bother me like it used to. I've learned to ignore him."

"Why don't you stand up to him?" she demanded. "He dumps on you, and you won't even defend yourself!"

"That's what he wants, and I refuse to give him the satisfaction. What did he say that has you so upset?"

She propped her chin in her hands. "How you aren't a very good mother because Frankie and I say whatever we want. He says we are rude and sarcastic!"

Farrel frowned. She doubted Ben would ever change. He didn't realize that he was alienating his daughters and that once they were out on their own, they might sever contact with him. He'd have no one to blame but himself. "I can't believe he would say that to you."

"I'm sick and tired of being around him. I don't want to see him anymore. He's never been a good father. All he does is screw up our lives. He hurts us, and he doesn't even care!"

Farrel patted Charly's shoulder. "That's just his way. I'll talk to him tomorrow," she promised. She doubted it would do any good, but she'd give it one last try for the girls' sakes.

<<<>>>

Frankie stared in disbelief at her sister. "Charly, why is Dad saying that about me and Mom?"

"He's jealous," she answered as she threw her magazine onto the floor.

"Of what?"

Charly looked at her sister. "How do I know? Probably because we turned out okay."

"That makes absolutely no sense," Frankie reasoned.

"Mom did everything for us. Dad never even tried to get to know us. He had nothing to do with how we turned out."

"I know," Charly replied. "But do you really think he's gonna give Mom any credit?"

Frankie sighed. "I know he won't, and it's stupid. He needs to grow up and act like a real father."

"What does a father act like?" Charly asked.

Frankie laughed.

Charly tossed her hair off her shoulder. "I'm serious." She stared into Frankie's eyes. "We have two examples — Dad and Robert. And we remember well what type of stepfather Robert turned out to be."

"I don't know what Dad's problem is," Frankie answered. "I wish I did. If he doesn't approve of us, then why force us to visit him all those summers?"

"I think it's a power trip for him," Charly said. "He used the child support money as a threat to Mom. If we don't do what he wants, then he won't help us."

"I don't care about his money, and Mom doesn't need it anymore," Frankie said.

"Yeah, but that's not the point. He should have willingly wanted to take care of us."

"But he'll never see it that way." Frankie's eyes narrowed.

"So, what do we do?"

"I don't know about you, Charly, but I'm just not gonna bother with him if he keeps putting us down. What's the point?"

"It's still stupid. He never treats us like he cares about us. He's always got something to complain about."

"Someday, maybe he'll look back and see what he's done. Maybe he'll regret it."

"Even if he does, he'll still twist it around and put the

blame on us."

"I know," Frankie said with a sigh as she sat on the edge of her sister's bed. Her eyes surveyed the messy room. "We know the truth, and that's all that matters." She looked at Charly. "So when you gonna clean up this mess?"

Charly yawned and then stretched. "What mess?" she asked, scanning the room.

<<<>>>

Farrel looked intently at her ex-husband. "Ben," she began, "Charly is upset because of the talk you had with her."

Ben shoved his hands into his pants pockets. "That girl has a problem with respect," he immediately replied.

Farrel took a moment before replying. "Can't you be a little less critical of the girls?"

"They don't appreciate anything. They want and keep expecting more."

"That's not true, Ben. They have both worked very hard in school—even through the rough times."

"And who's fault was that?" he asked critically.

"Meaning?" Farrel steeled herself for what she knew was coming. He'd dredge up every mistake she'd ever made.

"Meaning your relationship with Robert."

The blood rushed to her face. "I also protected them and removed them from that situation, didn't I?" Her tension built, and she fought back the urge to tell him what she really thought of him.

"You should have taught them to show respect," Ben persisted.

"Frankie and Charly have always been respectful. I have taught them to show respect for others, but have also taught them that they should be respected in return."

"What you have taught them, Farrel, is to have no respect

for me," he said harshly. "I'm their father, and I deserve respect without question."

"Look, Ben, I have never interfered with your relationship with the girls. I've sent you clippings of everything they've ever been involved in, and have kept you abreast of everything going on in their lives." Her eyes narrowed. "I can't believe that you could accuse me of this." She clenched her hands into tight balls, hoping to calm herself before she exploded.

"I call it as I see it," he calmly answered.

"I see it's no use talking to you." She turned to leave, then stopped. "I just have one more thing to say to you, Ben. And I hope you'll think long and hard about it."

"What's that?" he asked with a smirk.

"Just remember the circumstances of our divorce. I never turned my back on my daughters." She didn't wait for his response as she firmly shut his hotel room door behind herself.

<<<>>>

Farrel tightly clutched her purse in her hands. "I had to see you today, Dr. Feldon. I'm sorry for the short notice."

"I'm happy to squeeze you in," Jerry Feldon replied. "Now fill me in on everything that's happened since your last visit. What's gotten you so upset?" he asked, leaning back in his chair.

"It's Ben Stuart," she spat out between clenched teeth, as though the mere mention of his name caused her to become even angrier.

"Ben? How'd the graduation party go?"

"Very well. It's the garbage Ben's trying to fill Charly with. She's got enough on her mind without his putting more on her."

Feldon studied her. "Farrel, why do you allow him to upset you?"

She sighed wearily. "I don't know. He knows the right buttons to push. I went out of my way to treat him well when he was here. And what did I get in return?" she asked as she flung her hands in the air. "Just being ridiculed to Charly. But that's not all. He's putting Frankie down to Charly, also." She shook her head in disgust. "He's trying to put a rift between the girls."

"What were the girls' reactions?"

"They're both upset, and want nothing more to do with him."

"Then he hasn't succeeded in causing a rift between them. You don't have to deal with Ben Stuart, Farrel. You are financially stable now, and you can cut him completely out of *your* life. The girls can decide if, in the future, they want a relationship with him. That's their decision."

"How can I cut him out? He never listens."

"He has no control over you, Farrel, and you have to let him know that. The more upset you become, the more power you give him." Feldon folded his hands.

Farrel looked at him quizzically. "I didn't let him see that I was upset. At least I don't think I did."

"Let me explain. What can your ex-husband possibly do to you? He has to pay child support for Charly. As far as Frankie is concerned, you've been supporting her since she turned eighteen, even though you could have gotten support for her until she graduated from college. She has her loans and scholarships, and you are helping her with her other college expenses. A year from now, in all probability, you should be financially secure with the new book coming out next spring."

"That's true," she admitted. "I can afford to take care of the girls and myself right now without Ben's assistance, but Charly's support does help. It's just that he makes me so angry."

"That's because you let him. My advice is to get on with your life. If Ben Stuart wants a relationship with his daughters, it is up to him. You've done more than was necessary to keep a relationship between him and the girls. Frankie and Charlie realize all you've done for them, and they'll never forget it. If they want to see their father, you don't need to be a part of it. They are both old enough to make the decision for themselves. Don't feel guilty, because the choice is theirs. He's the one at fault, not you. Just remember that."

She smiled. "You make it sound so simple."

He returned her smile. "It is. When you have all of this confronting you at once, it's hard to look at it objectively. But you need to learn to stand back and look at it, analyze it, and then realize that no matter what you do, you can't change Ben. Only Ben can change Ben. The only thing you two have in common is the girls. There is nothing else. He is part of your past, and if he chooses to throw away his role as a father, he has only himself to blame."

"But he always throws my mistakes back at me."

"Of course, he does! It's easier to fault you than to face his own faults. He refuses to take responsibility for his own actions, and until he does, he's going to be a very lonely, unhappy man."

"That makes sense. Now, if I just remember what you've told me."

"Engrave it in your memory," he teased.

"I may just have to," Farrel said with a smile.

"Now tell me what's happening in the other areas of your life."

"The phone calls have tapered off."

"Do you still have the phone tap?" the doctor asked.

"Yes, but the caller doesn't stay on the line long enough to be positively identified. I'll be relieved when it's over, and they catch whoever is doing this."

"Do you still think it's Robert?"

"I do, but he may be growing tired of it. Hopefully, he'll stop." Farrel smiled weakly. "There's always something to intrude on my otherwise happy life."

"You're referring to your personal life?" Dr. Feldon asked.

Farrel blushed. "I am."

"How is everything going with Kyle?"

"He makes me happy."

"How does he treat you?"

"I couldn't ask for a kinder, more gentle man. But a part of me is still apprehensive."

"You need to give him a chance, Farrel. Only you can judge his character. Remember, just because you've had two bad relationships doesn't mean that Kyle will turn out to be another bad choice."

"I know." Her eyes brightened. "He makes me feel special, and sometimes I feel just like a teenager falling in love for the first time."

<<<>>>

"Where are the girls tonight?" Kyle asked.

"Frankie's out with Gary and Charly's at the Zakers'."

"So it's just you and me, kid," he teased.

Farrel smiled as she leaned back, resting her head against his shoulder. "This is nice. Just being able to relax and not think about anything."

"What about being loved and protected for the rest of your life?" he asked softly.

She sighed. "Twice I thought I was going to be loved and protected for the rest of my life, and look what happened."

211

"I know that it's not easy for you to completely trust a man, Farrel. But I'm patient, and you're worth waiting for." He hugged her close. "I hope that someday I can make you forget all that hurt. I will protect you and love you for the rest of your life."

She stiffened.

"Did I say something wrong?" he softly asked. "I thought I'd already told you how I feel, and you told me that you have feelings for me."

"No...I'm still upset over Ben." She touched his cheek. "I do have feelings for you, Kyle."

He inhaled deeply as he leaned forward. "Maybe your feelings for me aren't as deep as I thought." He looked into her eyes.

She couldn't escape his beautiful eyes penetrating her own. She turned, trying to look away but couldn't. Her heart quickened. "I do care," she whispered. "I care more than you could ever know." Tears filled her eyes.

"Then share your pain with me," he said, stroking her hair. "I want to know every part of you. I need to share your joys and sorrows. Let me in, Farrel. You started to the other night, but never finished."

A tear fell from her eye.

Kyle pulled her towards him, gently kissed her, and then cradled her in his arms. "I'll never hurt you or let anyone hurt you again. I promise."

Farrel knew his words were sincere, and it suddenly dawned on her how difficult it must be for him having to deal with her baggage. She needed no further proof of his sincerity. "Kyle, I can't deny my feelings for you. I'm just so afraid."

"Don't be," he said quickly. "I love and accept every part of you...past, present, and, hopefully, a future with me."

He cupped her face in his hands. "Tell me that you love me, Farrel," he said, searching her face. "I want to hear you say it."

"You know that I do," she whispered.

"I want to hear you say the words," he insisted.

She swallowed the lump in her throat. "I do...I do love you, Kyle," she choked as tears flowed freely from her eyes.

He kissed away the tears on her chin, cheeks, then lips as all of the bottled up emotions inside of Farrel came rushing out. It felt good to be in Kyle's arms. They stayed that way for several minutes until the phone rang, jarring them both.

It rang several times before Farrel grabbed it. "Maybe it's one of the girls."

Kyle watched as a strange expression came over her face. He put his head close to hers as he listened with her to the voice on the other end of the line. The voice was raspy and almost incoherent, making it obvious that the caller was disguising his identity. Kyle strained to make out what the caller was saying. He motioned to Farrel to keep the caller talking. She hoped this time she could keep him talking long enough for the call to be traced. She shuddered as the voice became threatening, and felt Kyle's arm slip around her waist. She was grateful he was with her.

"I warned you, Farrel. Now you have to pay for what you've done!" the voice hissed.

An eerie feeling crept over Farrel, sending chills down her spine. She looked desperately at Kyle. He pointed to his wristwatch. She knew that she needed to stall for time, and even though she didn't want to engage the caller in conversation, she knew she had to. "What...what did I do?" she asked in a shaky voice. "Tell me what I've done."

"He's there right now with you, isn't he?"

"Who?"

"Don't play games with me, Farrel."

Farrel looked questioningly at Kyle, and he again pointed to his wristwatch.

"I'm alone," she answered. "There's no one here with me."

"Liar!" the voice snarled.

"I'm telling you the truth. There is no one here but me. Why would I lie to you?"

"That's all you know how to do. I don't think you've ever told the truth one day in your life. He's there. I know he's there with you right now!" the voiced snarled.

"Who do you think is here?"

"Your boyfriend! The cop, that's who."

"No. No one is here. I told you I'm alone." Farrel chewed her bottom lip as she looked at Kyle, hoping the trace would go through.

"Don't lie to me! You know I can't stand liars. I'm losing patience with you. You'll be sorry for lying, you bitch!"

"I'm not lying. How many times do I have to tell you that?"

"Farrel, listen, and listen good. I'm only going to say this once."

"What?"

"Your days are numbered." He paused. "I'm coming for you."

Her palm grew sweaty, and she almost dropped the phone. "Who are you?" she demanded, trying to keep her voice steady.

"It doesn't matter. You've hurt too many people, and you have to be stopped. I intend to stop you."

"Who have I hurt?"

"Your lies are going to stop!" he hissed. "Do you hear me?"

Farrel looked helplessly at Kyle. Kyle pointed to the time and gave a thumbs up. Farrel slammed the phone down and turned to him. He quickly picked up the phone and made a call.

Farrel sank onto the sofa and waited for Kyle to join her. Could this nightmare finally be over? She hoped so. All she'd ever wanted was a normal life, and maybe now her wish would come true. She glanced at Kyle. He set the phone down, and seconds later, it began ringing again.

"Answer it, Farrel," he urged. "If it's Robert, don't worry. The previous call came from his phone. We got him."

Relief flooded through Farrel. She picked up the phone. "Hello?"

"Don't you *ever* hang up on me again!" the voice hissed.

"Say what you want to," Kyle whispered.

"I'm not afraid of you," she said confidently.

"You should be. You better keep a close eye on your daughters, too!"

"I know who you are."

The caller laughed sarcastically. "I don't think so."

"I know it's you, Robert. The police know it, too."

There was a brief period of silence, followed by the phone being slammed down.

Farrel quietly replaced the receiver and then turned to Kyle.

He put his arm around her. "It's finally over."

"Why would Robert do this to me?" she asked. "Why, after all this time? It doesn't make sense."

Kyle shook his head. "He didn't want to lose his control over you."

They both turned when they heard the door slam. Seconds later, Frankie and Charly walked into the room. "What's the matter, Mom?" Frankie looked at Kyle, then back to her mother.

"You look like you just saw a ghost," Charly said as she threw her jacket over the back of a chair.

"Hi, girls," Kyle said.

"Hi," they answered simultaneously.

"Will one of you please tell us what's going on?" Frankie demanded.

Kyle leaned forward. "Your mother received another phone call a little while ago. She was able to keep the caller on the line long enough to get a trace, and the police are on their way over to arrest him as we speak."

"Robert?" Frankie asked.

Kyle nodded. "Yes."

"I knew it was him!" Charly exclaimed.

"I hope they lock him up for the rest of his life," Frankie said bitterly. "He deserves it after what he's put us through."

"I've got to make a call," Kyle said.

While he made his call, Farrel turned her attention to her daughters. "This is low even for Robert. I can't believe he would do this to us."

"I can," Frankie said firmly. "He's sick."

Minutes later, Kyle walked back over to them. "I've got some news."

Farrel noted the bewildered expression on his face. "What is it?" she asked. "They got Robert, didn't they, Kyle?"

"Let's all sit down." He led Farrel to the sofa and sat next to her. Charly and Frankie sat on the loveseat facing them. They all looked at Kyle expectantly.

"Farrel, you need to go to the station to sign some papers."

"Sure," she nodded.

"I'll take you in a few minutes, but first I have to tell you something." Kyle's brow furrowed.

"What?" she asked. "They have Robert, don't they?"

He shook his head in disbelief. "It's not Robert, Farrel. Your ex-husband wasn't making those phone calls to you."

"What?!" she exclaimed. "But you said the call was traced to his house."

"It was," he explained. "But Robert had nothing to do with the phone calls. It's been Bobby from the beginning."

Farrel's hand flew to her mouth. "Bobby? Why?"

The girls sat in stunned silence.

"I know it's difficult to comprehend. The kid must be pretty messed up, but he will be booked."

"Can I talk to him when we get to the station?" Farrel asked.

"I don't think that would be a good idea, Farrel."

"See if you can arrange it," she insisted.

"I'll try," Kyle promised. "But what do you hope to accomplish?"

"I need to know why."

Chapter Twelve

Farrel sat in a conference room waiting for Bobby to be brought in. The room was cramped and stuffy, with peeling paint visible on almost every wall. The ceiling was stained with watermarks, and the large table in the center of the room was badly scarred.

The door opened, and Farrel turned to face her former stepson as he was led into the room. She was shocked by his looks, and couldn't believe that this was the same boy she had known. His features had grown hard, and his long hair looked like it hadn't been shampooed in weeks. His clothes were rumpled and dirty. He stood stone faced, and his eyes flitted wildly back and forth. Robert stood by his side.

"Hi, Bobby," Farrel said softly.

He raised his eyes to hers but said nothing.

Robert put a hand on his son's shoulder, glaring angrily at her. "It's your fault he's in this mess."

"No, Robert, it's not my fault." She looked again at Bobby "On second thought, maybe you're right. It is my fault for not insisting that he get the help he needed years ago."

"How dare you. There's nothing wrong with my son!" Robert thundered.

"Keep it down, please," Kyle ordered with a sharp look pointed at Robert.

Robert turned on his heel, facing Kyle. "You have no right to tell me what to do! You're nothing but a home wrecker—stealing another man's wife."

Kyle shook his head. "Robert, you and Farrel are divorced. She's free to do as she pleases."

Robert's eyes flashed angrily, but he kept silent.

Farrel put a hand on Bobby's shoulder, and he thrust it off. "What do you want from me?" he snarled.

"I just want to know why. Why have you tormented me and the girls for all these months?"

He glared at her. "You deserved it."

"No, Bobby. Deep down, you know that we didn't deserve what you did to us. You terrified us." She paused as she studied him. "Please tell me why you really did it. That's all I want to know."

"You left my father," he mumbled.

She raised her eyebrows. "Yes, I did, and you know why."

He rapidly blinked. "You left me with him!" he screamed, whirling on his heel. With clenched fists, he rushed at Robert and pounded on his chest.

Kyle grabbed the boy's shoulders and then held Bobby's arms behind his back.

"Don't you hurt my son!" Robert ordered.

Kyle eyed Robert coldly. "It looks like you already have."

<<<>>>

"I'm glad this mess is finally over!" Charly exclaimed. "But I sort of feel sorry for Bobby."

"Me, too," Frankie agreed. "What do you think will happen to him, Mom?"

"He'll definitely get the help he needs, and then maybe Robert will finally accept responsibility for his part in this," Farrel replied. "He also needs help."

"It's still too bad," Frankie said. "But at least Bobby will have the chance to deal with all the years of abuse from his father."

"It'll take a long time, honey. That poor kid has years of pain welled up inside."

"But why did he make those calls?" Charly asked.

Farrel sighed. "He wanted to punish me for leaving him."

"That doesn't make sense, Mom," Frankie reasoned.

"It does if you think about it. When we lived with them, Robert had me to thrust his abuse on, and then you girls. Bobby was given a reprieve. Robert had convinced himself that he had never abused his son, and went to the opposite extreme by giving in to his every whim and lavishing all kinds of attention on him." Farrel clasped her hands together. "When we left, Robert only had his son, so he started abusing him again. Bobby went from abuse, to love, and back to abuse."

"That's weird," Frankie said sadly.

"Yes, it is. Just imagine the confusion going on in Bobby's mind all these years. Eventually, something had to snap."

"Why did he treat you like crap and always tell Robert to dump you?" Charly asked.

"I'm no psychiatrist, but I think it was to assure Robert that he was on his side. Bobby knew Robert would never leave on his own accord, so it was the perfect response."

"Will Robert have charges filed against him?" Charly asked.

"I don't know, honey. It's hard to say how the system will work in this case. But I'm certain that he'll be forced into counseling. Maybe then he'll finally admit what he did to all of us and that the consequences of his life are his own doing."

"I'm just relieved that he won't be bothering us anymore," Frankie stated.

"Amen to that," Farrel said.

<<<>>>

Betty dabbed her mouth with a napkin. "It's so unbelievable. Like something right out of a novel!" she exclaimed. "My heart goes out to that poor boy."

Farrel looked intently at her. "I just wish I would have done something way back when the school called me."

"What could you have possibly done, Farrel?"

"I don't know," she admitted. "I should have never let Robert abuse any of us. I never dreamed that he'd been abusing his own son," She ran a hand through her hair. "When I first met Robert, I never picked up on anything. I should have done something," she repeated.

"Mom, you were lucky you could protect yourself," Charly said.

"Yeah. Besides, we all thought he was treating Bobby okay," Frankie replied.

"Well, why didn't the school do something?" Farrel asked disgustedly.

"Farrel, what more could they do? You said yourself that Bobby denied any abuse from his father," Betty said.

"It just makes me sick to my stomach." She clenched her teeth tightly together. "At least he'll now get the help he needs."

"And Robert will finally get what's coming to him," Betty said.

"It won't be too soon for me," she said. "I still think someone should have helped that kid."

Betty stared thoughtfully at Farrel.

"What?" Farrel asked.

"I want you to think about something for a moment."

"What?"

221

"You acted no differently than Bobby did."

Farrel was puzzled. "I don't follow you."

Betty looked thoughtfully at her. "How many times did you refuse to press charges against Robert? How many times did you cover for him?"

Her face reddened. Betty was right, and she had no response.

"You lied to me from day one—the day in the garden. You told me that you were clumsy and incurred your bruises from bumping into objects."

"But I…." She feebly tried to justify her lies but knew she couldn't. Betty had spoken the truth, and the truth hurt.

"Is it any different?" Betty asked gently.

Her shoulders drooped. "No, it isn't. I never knew one person could scare me so much. Bobby lived with that fear day in and day out, before I met Robert, and after I left him."

"There *is* something to be thankful for, though," Betty said.

"What?"

"Bobby will get the help he needs, and hopefully, it will save him from being a future abuser."

Farrel nodded. "It'll take a long time for him to come to terms with everything that's happened to him."

"Yes, but at least he now has a chance for a happy future. That's all that matters," Betty said.

<<<>>>

"So, where are the four of you headed tonight?" Kyle asked the group no one in particular.

"Frankie and I are going school clothes shopping," Gary said with a trace of laughter in his voice.

Frankie playfully punched his shoulder. "Hey! You said you would show me what the girls in college are wearing."

Kyle laughed heartily. "Get used to it, Gary. Once they get you, they make you do all kinds of things you never dreamed you'd be doing."

"What do you mean by that, Detective?" Farrel jokingly asked.

"Whoa, looks like I got myself in hot water again," Kyle teased.

"Again!" Farrel exclaimed. "You haven't been out of hot water since I met you."

Charly laughed. "You guys are so weird."

"And what are your thoughts, Morrison?" Kyle asked.

"Don't drag me into this. I'm staying neutral," he grinned.

"Sure, Morrison, play it safe," Gary said.

"That's my motto. Don't take sides."

"So, how's Lisa doing?" Farrel asked.

"Good. She's going to live with our mother and go to college in California."

"I sure miss her," Frankie said.

"Yeah, it's strange without her around," Morrison said, then added with a glint of mischief in his eye, "but it sure is great being able to use the bathroom."

"I know what you mean," Kyle jumped in. "The women go in there, and you can never get them out."

"Morrison, now look what you've started," Charly said, and then grinned.

"Well, we women are going to make a list of all the things you guys do that make us crazy," Farrel said.

"You start the list, Mom, and we'll add to it when we get home," Frankie said.

<<<>>>

"Peace and quiet at last," Kyle sighed, leaning back into the sofa.

"You could have had peace and quiet sooner if you hadn't gotten the boys so wound up, you instigator," Farrel teased.

"They're a great group of kids."

"That, they are. It's a relief to see the girls so relaxed again."

"With all your daughters and you have been through the past few years, you must feel a tremendous burden lifted from your shoulders."

Farrel sighed deeply. "It does feel good. Now I can finally put the past behind me and get on with my life."

"Just so I'm included in your present and future," Kyle said seriously.

"You know you are, Kyle. I don't know how I would have gotten through these past weeks without you to lean on."

"And it wasn't so bad to lean on me, was it?"

Farrel smiled. "No, it wasn't. As a matter of fact, I could get used to having you around." She slipped her arm through his and looked into his eyes. "I've gotten used to having you around."

"That's what I like to hear." He stroked her cheek. "So, when are you planning your trip?"

She frowned. "I'm not sure. I wanted to go the end of July, but Frankie won't be too thrilled leaving Gary. He has to be back in school a couple of weeks before she starts, so I might plan it then."

"Where's your destination?"

"I'm not sure of that either. I'm letting the girls decide."

"I have some vacation time coming myself," he hinted.

"Is that so?" Farrel grinned. "What do you plan to do?"

Kyle shrugged. "I don't know. Find an attractive author and see if she can help a lonely detective fill a void in his life."

She chuckled. "If that's a hint, Detective Haley, it's pretty shallow." She squeezed his hand. "For your information, the girls and I have already discussed the possibility of you joining us. They like you."

"And what was the verdict?"

"A unanimous yes!"

He smiled. "I don't know what I'm going to do with you. Were you ever going to tell me?"

"Yes, I was, but first I wanted to see if you really wanted to go with us."

"I would go to the end of the world for you." He gently turned her chin until she was facing him. He gazed into her eyes. "One thing I promise you, Farrel, is that no one will ever hurt you again. You need to believe that. I will be that character in your book — the one who loves you more than his own life. That is my promise to you."

She kissed him tenderly. "I don't just love you. I've fallen in love with you, Kyle. The way I feel about you I've never felt for another man," she whispered.

A smile spread across his face. "You don't know how long I've waited to hear you say that, Farrel." He cradled her in his arms. "I'm going to show you and the girls what a normal family is really like. I'll smother the three of you with so much love and affection that you'll forget all the pain and suffering you went through. That's my promise."

"I accept," she said as tears filled her eyes.

Susan K. Droney
AUTHOR

Writing is Susan's number one passion. When she isn't writing, she enjoys reading, spending time in her garden, and visiting family and friends. She has many novels, short stories, and magazine articles to her credit. Raised in western New York, she now resides in New Jersey. For information about Susan's current and upcoming titles, please visit http://www.susandroney.com or http://susandroney.blogspot.com